YES, AND

A NOVEL

CINDY GUNDERSON

CHAPTER 1

Typical, she thinks. Rowena always takes the best parking spot—marked *Guest,* mind you—without any thought or consideration for others. Who does she think she is? *Is her time more valuable than mine?*

"But I have hip pain," Jo can almost hear her protesting in her sickly sweet, frail voice.

"Don't we all!" she would bark in response. Rowena should have to hobble up the sidewalk like the rest of us. And if that's truly as painful as she says, then she should stay home. *Like the rest of us.*

Letting the blinds snap back into place, Jo slumps into the sofa, crossing her soft arms across her doughy chest. Maybe I'm being unfair, she thinks. Pondering this possibility, she is entranced momentarily by the rhythmic movements of her grey, feline clock on the opposite wall.

Eventually, she shakes her head as her hand presses into the worn arm of the sofa, forcing her unwilling body to an upright position.

"It's as good a time as ever for breakfast," she comments to the perpetually wide-eyed time-keeper, as she shuffles toward the kitchen. Her soft, white hair stands on end above her right ear, but she isn't aware of that yet this morning. She also isn't aware that she left a tv stand just slightly askew the night before, and now it catches her knee as she passes through the door. Luckily, her arm shoots out, bracing her weight against the solid wooden doorframe, allowing her to remain upright.

"That's unfortunate, isn't it?" she mutters, giving a spiteful kick to the stand, knocking it to the floor. "Yet I'm still standing, and you..." she glances at the fallen stand and a crackly laugh bursts from her, the sound somewhat of a rarity these days.

Continuing in her forward trajectory, she eventually makes it to the kitchen and is surprised by a soft, purring creature moving between her ankles.

"Precious!" she coos, her mood immediately softening as she adjusts her glasses in order to view the fluffy, white cat clearly. "I didn't know you were up already. Would you like some breakfast, too?"

Precious purrs in appreciation, her smashed face staring up at Jo as she paces between her food bowl and Jo's slippered feet.

"Alright, alright, give me a second," she croons, opening the cupboard door and pulling out the closest can of organic, grain-free, wet cat food. The counter is littered with glasses, mugs, and platters that can't quite be returned to their proper places, due to the height of the shelves and the shortness of Jo's legs. Though, as long as her favorite spot next to the sink is available, she doesn't much mind the clutter.

Pulling the ancient can opener from the drawer, she wriggles the blade into place along the metal lip. After a brief struggle, the lid gives way, and the smell of tuna fills the kitchen.

"Such an impatient kitty," Jo comments adoringly, placing

the now overflowing dish on the floor. Seeing the food, Precious immediately turns her back on Jo and begins lapping up the soft meat, her fluffy tail moving in serpentine swirls along the stained linoleum.

Precious will be the only living thing that Jo talks with today, and that is just how she prefers it. Besides the workers that check in on her every week and the occasional doctor's appointment, Jo doesn't have to interact with anyone.

Perhaps if the workers were sociable, that sort of human contact would be more enjoyable. Or if the doctor didn't continually spout off about her losing weight, she may actually look forward to those monthly visits. As it currently stands, she finds both horrendously annoying.

The problem is, she thinks, nobody actually cares a lick about my opinion, or—heaven forbid—what I might want. They all nod and tilt their heads while they listen, but they are simply biding time—enduring my answers—until the moment comes when they can tell me exactly what decisions to make and how to perceive the world. I've spent far too many years being told what to do. I'm definitely not going to spend the last few good years I have left *losing the same ten pounds over and over again.*

Ambling back to her armchair, she sits, and her stomach immediately lets out a low growl. Cursing her distractibility, she rolls her eyes and again presses her arm into the sofa rest. Laboriously lifting herself to her feet, she retraces her steps on the path to the kitchen, glancing victoriously at the TV stand as she passes.

CHAPTER 2

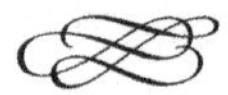

A hesitant knock on the door startles Jo. She had been enjoying her morning nap with *Days of Our Lives* playing in the background. Typically, she wouldn't actually sleep until after the program ended, but such is life at the age of eighty-seven.

I'm not getting up, she thinks, shifting her weight on the sofa. People should really take a moment to read the 'no soliciting' sign before wasting their time trying to sell Girl Scout cookies or cleaning products at this door. Pulling the faded quilt up to her chin, she focuses on the flashing screen.

The knock sounds again, slightly more insistent this time around. Jo's nostrils flare as she belligerently stares at the hazy, romanticized image of Brady leading Kristen to the door of his parent's townhome for an introduction.

"That's a terrible idea," Jo gripes under her breath, knowing full-well that Brady can't hear her through the tube. Regardless, her television predictions bring her an inordinate amount of satisfaction. Especially when they come to fruition.

Another—almost tired—knock breaks her concentration.

"Jo? I know you're in there. Please open the door," a muffled voice calls through the door, barely audible to Jo's ears above the dialogue between Brady and his insufferable mother.

Sighing resignedly, Jo hoists herself to a sitting position. "I'm not wearing pants," she announces, as if issuing a challenge.

"You usually aren't," the woman retorts, exasperated.

Pushing off from the sofa, Jo makes her way to the door and unlocks it tentatively. Twisting the handle, she pulls the door open just a smidge and observes the stranger through the storm glass.

"Who are you?" she questions charily through the inch of open space.

The young woman on the step deflates instantaneously, her eyes—puffy and lined with exhaustion—drop to stare at her Mary Jane's.

Her pathetic appearance causes Jo pause. She clears her throat before addressing the girl again. "Are you selling something?" she asks finally, her tone devoid of any outright antagonism for the moment.

"No," the woman breathes, twisting her fingers around a tissue. "I'm here to check on you," she explains, her eyes lifting again and hesitating at Jo's naked thighs.

"From Simply Living? I don't need to be checked on," Jo retorts, her voice low and accusatory. "Every time one of you people comes over, I end up missing something."

"I know you think—"

"I don't think, *I know*. I set my porcelain bell on that end table *right there*," Jo insists, flinging the door wide and pointing next to the sofa. "Then someone from Simply Living 'stopped by to check on me' and it was gone."

The woman nods. "I wish I knew what happened to it, Jo, but we've asked everyone there—"

"Of course he wouldn't admit to it," she snaps.

Pursing her lips, the woman steps toward the glass. "May I come in, please?"

Jo inspects her face. There's something familiar about this one, but she can't quite place it. She probably stopped by months ago.

Giving in, she pushes the door forward to allow the woman entrance. "If you're here to tell me I need to clean up...don't," she mutters, moving back to her favorite seat on the sofa and wrapping the quilt protectively around her waist. "I like my townhome as-is."

"I'm not here to *tell* you anything," the woman asserts, "I'm simply here to see that you're getting along."

"Huh," Jo answers, her eyebrows furrowed. "I'm not sure I believe that, considering the other visits of late." Giving her a once-over, she can't help but ask, "Have you been here before?"

"I have," the woman answers, "but it's been a while. And I'm kind of forgettable," she admits, a sad smile on her lips.

Something about how the woman's shoulders cave in on themselves and how she almost disappears in the chair makes Jo feel the smallest twinge of guilt over the way she treated her on the step. Though not typically a hostess, she rises, dropping her blanket, and moves toward the kitchen.

"Would you like some tea?"

"Oh, you don't need to put any on for me," she responds dismissively.

"It's not for you. I want tea and didn't want to be rude," Jo alleges.

"Well I'll have some then," the woman agrees, obviously pleased as she folds her hands in her lap.

Attempting to ignore the clatter Jo is making in the kitchen, the young woman quickly surveys the living room. A dirty plate sits on the coffee table. That could be from this morning, she thinks, continuing to scan. The threadbare rug needs replacing and the windows are abysmally dirty, but other than that...it seems mostly tidy, actually.

A TV stand seems to have been forgotten on the floor, and she stands quickly to right it, propping it against the wall. She smiles as she again takes her seat on the sofa, grateful that she won't need to have another awkward conversation with Jo about appropriately sanitary living conditions. The last one didn't go over well.

A whistle sounds from the other room, and the sound of water pouring into mugs reaches her ears. How long has it been since Jo offered me tea? I must have caught her in a good mood, she thinks.

Amused at her good fortune, she calls out, "Jo, anything I can do to help you in there?"

"No need, I can handle it perfectly well myself, thank you," Jo responds brusquely. A moment later, she dodders into the living room with a small tray balanced in her hands.

Before Jo has a chance to cross the rug, the girl stands abruptly and relieves her of the tray, setting it on the coffee table. Jo stands stock-still with her arms outstretched, attempting to process what just occurred.

Not willing to acknowledge that she stepped on Jo's toes, the young woman quickly distracts herself by preparing her tea. Eventually, Jo joins her on the sofa, not bothering to cover her legs with the quilt this time. Gingerly, Jo picks up a spoon and scoops a healthy serving of sugar into her tea and stirs it, her spoon clinking melodically on the edge of the mug.

The woman observes her out of the corner of her eye, intrigued. How can she possibly look dainty holding that spoon, when only ten minutes ago, that would have been the last adjective she'd have used to describe her behavior?

"So," Jo starts, cupping the beverage between her palms,

her hands absorbing the warmth, before taking a sip. "Are you satisfied that I'm doing just fine for myself?"

A surprised laugh escapes the woman's lips mid-sip. "I'm not sure I can determine that simply by sitting in your living room," she replies, setting her cup on the tray.

"And why not?" Jo asks, befuddled. "I've kept the place tidy, I'm eating three meals a day—"

"I can't verify that," she repeats, waggling her finger, but Jo waves her off.

"You can obviously see that I'm even taking good care of Precious—"

"That's right, Precious!" the girl interrupts, grinning. "I haven't seen her yet. Where's she gotten off to?"

"She's skeptical of strangers, and I don't blame her," Jo answers, shooting a meaningful look over the top of her mug.

"Well," the girl sighs contentedly. "Hopefully she'll make an appearance. I've always liked that cat."

"Hmph," Jo grunts, setting her tea on the table and settling back into the cushion. "As I was saying, it's clear that I'm capable of taking care of myself."

"Based on my very preliminary assessment," the woman emphasizes, "I would tend to agree. Though I do need to take a look in your bedroom at some point."

Jo sighs, "You and me both."

"What do you mean by that?" she asks, crossing her legs.

"I haven't been there in weeks," Jo says.

"But the last time I was here, you were excited about that new bed you were buying—what was it? A mahogany sleigh bed or something like that?"

Jo nods.

"Did something happen with the delivery?" The woman reaches for her cellphone. "I can look into that if you'd like—"

"No," Jo stops her, shifting her weight on the cushion. "It came, but—" she pauses, looking at the table as if suddenly distracted by a small insect. "It's too tall," she finally admits.

"Too tall?"

"Too tall!" Jo repeats, chagrined. "I can't—it's too high for me to climb up on the mattress."

The girl's head cocks to one side in bewilderment. "Will you show me?" she asks.

"It's nothing to get your panties in a twist about," Jo insists. "I rather enjoy sleeping on the couch—"

"You've been sleeping on the couch?"

"It's a life choice!" Jo asserts, throwing up her hands in exasperation.

"I'm not convinced that counts as a choice, Jo. There has to be something we can do to solve the problem, right? It just seems silly to sleep out here when you've got a nice bed available," she cajoles. When Jo doesn't meet her eyes, she sets her mug again on the tray and stands. "Just show it to me," she commands, placing a hand on her hip.

"I've already gotten off this couch three times in the last hour. I'm sure you can find it on your own," Jo says stubbornly, settling deeper into the cushion.

The girl's arms instinctively fold as she turns and walks lightly into the kitchen and through the door into Jo's bedroom. The only bathroom in the townhome is located through here, as well, and she quickly takes a peek. Samples of skincare creams and makeup litter the counter, but it looks to be clean underneath the clutter.

Turning, she takes in the behemoth in front of her. Jo wasn't kidding. The bed, while of gorgeous workmanship, takes up nearly all of the space in the room. A beautiful floral quilt sits on top, the corners neatly tucked, with three perfectly fluffed throw pillows adorning the head of the bed. Precious—comfortably perched atop the middle cushion—

lifts her head, perturbed. It's not likely that Jo prepared this bed on her own. Perhaps an aide from Simply Living took care of this for her?

"Looks quite inviting," she comments to Precious under her breath as she hoists herself onto the bed. Precious immediately yowls in complaint at being jostled, flashes her perpetual scowl in the woman's direction, and jumps to the floor. Slinking into the closet, she promptly burrows into a pile of clothes and disappears.

It wasn't *that* difficult to get up here, the woman thinks, but then remembers how slowly Jo moved to the kitchen earlier. Jumping down to the floor, she smooths the comforter back to its pristine condition, not wanting to give Jo any reason to accuse her of ruining her things. Again.

On her path back to the living room, she quickly inspects the kitchen. Her eyes widen at the sheer number of bowls, containers, and appliances crowded on the counters.

"Jo, how in the world did you make tea with all of this in your way?" she questions sincerely.

"You get used to it," Jo calls.

"Can I help you put them away?" the woman offers, opening a cupboard and looking for empty space.

"If I'm a little shorter on one end to reach, you're even worse off."

"But maybe we could rearrange things in here so you could access them? Put them at a lower level?"

"Don't touch my cupboards."

"I think it would make it better. Then you could use your counters again, wouldn't that be nice?"

Jo sighs, refusing to grace that comment with a response.

"I guess, at a minimum, we could get you a decent stepstool. Actually, that would solve the bed problem, too!" the woman continues, her tone lilting with excitement. Peeking her head around the corner, she attempts to catch Jo's attention, a childlike grin on her thin lips.

"Would you like me to take care of that for you, Jo?" she asks.

Jo continues to watch Marlena brood on the television screen in front of her, not even glancing toward the kitchen.

"Jo? Have I said something wrong?" she asks, her eyebrows furrowing in disappointment. "I only meant—"

"Thank you for checking in on me," Jo says blandly, her eyes still glued to the set.

"I—" the girl starts, then thinks better of it. Standing stiffly in the doorway, she straightens her shirt. "I'll let myself out. Maybe we could discuss this next time?" she asks hopefully.

Jo is clearly no longer listening and gives zero reaction as the woman lifts her purse to her shoulder and slips out the front door.

CHAPTER 3

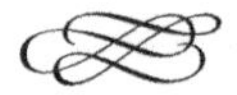

"I think it could be a good change," Toby argues, leaning on the half wall between Clara's living room and kitchen. "It just wasn't a good fit."

"Toby, you can't possibly think that taking a leave of absence will end well? Everyone I know who has left their schooling mid-way never ends up going back. It's too difficult to get back in the swing of things," Clara insists, her hands gesticulating wildly, despite the fact that one of them is holding a spatula.

"But the thing is, it feels too difficult *now*. If it's 'difficult' to get into the swing of things as-is, then it's kind of the same diff' isn't it?" Toby reasons, his long, unruly curls shaking around his face.

"No, Toby, I don't think it is," Clara sighs. "And you're so close to finishing. Don't you only have three semesters left?" She turns to the stove, stirring the sausage with intensity, grease popping on the front of her striped apron. "Can't you just suck it up for another year?"

"You're right, Clar, I never thought of that."

She rolls her eyes, exhaling loudly.

Toby watches her, pushing his dark, boxy glasses further up the bridge of his nose, not sure what to say next. Turning from the kitchen, he inspects the single, framed print on Clara's living room wall—a large landscape of the English countryside. He takes a deep breath, shoving his hands in his pockets. She has always disapproved of his choices. Literally all of them. Even when they were kids and he would choose a movie to watch, or which restaurant they would go to, it was never the 'right' option as far as she was concerned. At a certain point, he thought he'd stopped caring.

As they got older, Clara became so involved with her friends and school activities that she rarely had time to comment on Toby's life. Once she moved to Portland, it became infinitely easier to pretend they had finally grown out of this dynamic. Somehow he had convinced himself that she would be able to see him as a grown adult now and respect his decisions as such. Apparently not.

"Have you at least gotten a job, then?" she calls.

Toby clenches his teeth.

"That's what I thought," Clara announces indignantly. "You're asking to stay here and you don't even have any plans?"

Toby turns and steps into the kitchen in time to watch her slide the sizzling sausage rounds to a plate next to the stove. Carefully, she wipes the edge of the pan with a cloth before returning it to the stovetop.

Pressing her palms into the counter, she closes her eyes and breathes deeply. "Toby, it's not that I don't believe you're capable of doing something else, or figuring this out on your own, it's just—"

"That you don't think I know what I'm getting into?" he finishes her sentence.

Turning to face him, her short hair sways around her jawline and she pushes her bangs aside to squarely meet his eyes.

"You think I'm that naive?" he asks.

"Well?" she asks, her hand moving to her hip. "You can't really blame me."

"You really have that little respect for me?" Toby asks, leaning on one of the four chairs surrounding the circular kitchen table.

"It's not about respect—"

"How's it not?"

"I'm just being practical! You haven't finished anything you've started since high school, and I *finally* thought you were going to! I know you might not be convinced that this program will lead to a job you'll enjoy, but it could've been a really solid back-up. It would allow you to make more than minimum wage, at least, while...figuring out whatever else it is you want to do."

"Is that how it's worked out for you?" he asks.

"It will!" Clara fires back, tossing the spatula into the sink. "And how dare you criticize my life when you're asking *me* for help?"

"I'm not, I'm simply pointing out that even a traditional path includes some risk," Toby pleads.

"What risk? I've got a fantastic internship and a part-time job. Not making a ton of money in the short-term isn't a risk. It's a necessary step to building value."

"I get that, but you also really believe in what you're doing. You're always talking about how I need to suffer through and finish something practical, but have you considered that you got lucky? The thing that you find interesting also happens to *be practical*. What if that wasn't the case? Would you do it anyway? I know I haven't finished my degree, but it's because it doesn't *feel* right. It's not connecting with me—"

"It's not luck, Toby. And a job doesn't have to 'connect with you', it just needs to pay the bills. At least in the short-term."

"But that's not how I want to live my life! I don't want to be Dad."

Clara's lips purse into a thin line at the mention of their father. "Dad did what he had to. He provided for our family, and he worked *hard* every day of his life so that we—"

"So that we—what?" Toby challenges. "So that we could follow in his footsteps and work hard every day of our lives doing something we hate? What's the point of that? So I can buy a nice tv someday? Dad was really good at bringing in money, and look how that worked out for him. As far as I can tell, having nice things didn't compensate for poor relationships. We could have spent those years before Mom passed actually being a happy family if Dad wasn't so tied to his work." He walks to stand next to her, leaning backward against the counter. Even when hunched, his tall, lanky frame towers over his sister's shorter one.

"Dad working a lot wasn't the cause of their divorce, Toby," Clara asserts, grabbing the serving plate from the counter and moving it to the table.

"But the stress could have been—"

"Don't even go there," Clara whispers. "There's nobody to blame for Mom's death."

"I know, I only meant—" he stops short after a warning glance from his sister. "I promise I'll find a way to help with rent."

"I don't plan on you living here long enough to have to help with rent," Clara quips, stomping toward him and opening a cupboard door directly next to his head, pulling two plates from the shelf.

Toby steps to the side. "Groceries then. And I know, only a couple of weeks," he insists.

"Uh-huh," she says, arranging their place settings. "Can you grab cups?"

Reaching behind her neck, she unties her apron and hangs it on the hook next to the back door.

Toby obediently finds two glasses and begins filling them from the fridge dispenser. "I promise, Clar."

Pulling her chair out, Clara sits, snatching a napkin from the stack in the middle of the table and folding it in her lap.

"You're the best sister a guy could ask for?" he searches, a cheesy grin on his face.

"Oh sit down already, it's going to get cold."

TAKING HER LAST BITE, Clara watches Toby as she chews. She notices the short beard he's started growing and the relaxed position of his body. It must be nice to be so easy-going in the midst of a complete breakdown, she thinks. I have trouble sleeping when I find a spelling error in a sent email.

"What do Carol and Dad think about this?" she asks, swallowing. Toby continues digging into his second helping, purposefully avoiding her gaze.

"Wait—they don't know, do they?" she says, her eyes widening with sudden realization. "Is that why you're staying here? I thought—"

"I'm going to tell them," he assures her calmly, wiping his mouth with a napkin. "I just...haven't found the right moment yet."

"Oh, I hate to spoil it for you, but there isn't going to *be* a right moment, Tob," she says, hastily rising from her chair and moving her dishes to the sink. Her chest tightens even imagining this potential conversation. When Toby remains maddeningly silent, she balls her hands into fists and shakes them at the back of his head.

"I know what you're doing back there," he says slowly, his mouth still full of food.

"I'm not doing anything," she shoots back, a little too quickly. Walking to the edge of the carpet, she announces, "I'm going to bed. Please do the dishes," then turns on her heel and stalks to her bedroom at the end of the hall.

Breathing a silent sigh of relief, Toby slowly lifts his last fork full of dinner to his mouth. This can't possibly be as catastrophic as she says, he thinks, mulling her comments over in his mind. At twenty-one years old, how can I be expected to know exactly what I want to do with my life? How is it not more normal to take some time to figure it out?

Sitting back in his chair, hands resting on his jeans, Toby stares at the wall. Somehow, two weeks ago the idea of moving to Portland and starting over sounded exciting. But was it just that *anything* would have sounded more exciting then stepping foot into another lecture hall? Should I have stayed in Madison? He ponders this for a moment. No, he thinks, coming to Portland isn't just about escaping. This city holds the last memories I have with my mom. I don't exactly know what I'm searching for, but I know it wasn't in the Midwest.

Shifting his chair, he looks out the window at the green trees—the evening light barely illuminating the yard—and smiles. Thinking of the student loan money still in his account, he reminds himself that he has the ability to be flexible. He could go back if things don't work out, so what's the harm in experimenting for a few months?

Standing, he pushes his chair neatly against the table and walks to the sink, filling it with warm, soapy water. Opening his phone with his dry hand, he queues up his favorite playlist, making sure to keep the volume low. The last thing he needs is to attract more of Clara's negative attention. As the steady rhythm fills the kitchen, Toby begins to scrub the dirty dishes. The job search—or maybe home search? —can start tomorrow.

CHAPTER 4

Precious makes her appearance in the living room shortly after the door shuts. Good instincts, this one, Jo thinks. Having already resumed her horizontal position on the couch, she reaches her arm out to stroke the fur between the cat's ears. Precious alights on Jo's blanket-covered chest, obstructing her view of the television. Instead of fighting it, Jo simply closes her eyes, gently laying her hand on Precious' vibrating body.

As the dialogue from the game show grows fuzzy in her semi-conscious state, Jo is transported back twenty years...

They were sitting across from each other at her favorite lunch spot, Victorianos. Every time Cheri would come out to visit Stillwater, they would go for lunch. Cheri continually tried to suggest trendy options in the Twin Cities, but Jo had a soft spot for this place.

"I don't really love eating heavy meals in the middle of the day," Cheri would argue, but Jo always insisted that she order the meatballs regardless. And Cheri always loved them. On this day, however, Cheri's typical good humor was absent.

After mostly moving the noodles around her plate for twenty minutes, she finally lifted her eyes.

"I think it's time for you to move, Mom," Cheri says, gently reaching across the table to touch her hand. "Closer to me."

"Ha. That's a good one."

"I'm serious."

Jo swallows and inspects her daughter across the table, Cheri's eyes pleading with her.

"But I love where I live," Jo responds, confusion on her face. "And I don't want to move all of my stuff."

"Well, that's part of the problem," Cheri admits, retracting her hand. "You have so much 'stuff' in your house that it's barely liveable. I know you don't want to hear this, but you're getting older. I just imagine you tripping on those boxes, or pieces of extra furniture. You could really hurt yourself."

"I'm getting along just fine," Jo insists, pulling her hand back to take another bite of al dente noodles.

Cheri pauses, folding her arms and leaning back against the booth seat. "I heard what happened," she admits softly.

"What do you mean 'what happened'? I fell, that's a normal thing to have 'happen,'" Jo brushes her off. "You fell down the stairs all the time as a kid."

"That's a little different, Mom," Cheri laughs. "Besides, if you moved next to me, we could see you all the time. We could do this," she motions at the table, "a few times a week if you wanted. And then you'd get to see the kids. They'd actually get to know you instead of only seeing pictures. And I found this great place—"

"I don't want to move, Cheri."

BUT SHE HAD MOVED. And then Cheri died of breast cancer a few years later. The kids had moved across the country to be with their Dad, and Jo was left alone in a city she barely knew.

CHAPTER 5

Clara props the door open to shake the rain off her coat, then steps inside and slips out of her soggy shoes. "How'd it go?" she asks, laying her things on the bench along the wall and walking up the stairs.

"Great," Toby calls from the kitchen. Sometimes he wonders if Clara regrets the decision to have him cook on her late nights instead of just ordering take-out. "It's your contribution," she had said initially, but looking around at the used pots, dirty towels, and spills on the counters, he isn't convinced he's contributing anything.

"Smells good," she comments, rounding the corner.

"Swiss steak."

Clara wrinkles her nose. "Isn't that what Dad used to make?"

Toby nods.

"The dish that Mom hated?"

He nods again.

"Then why are you making it?"

Shrugging, he moves a pot holder to the table, then turns

to lift the small, cast-iron dish from the stove. "I don't know, I was at the store and saw the tenderized steak—"

"You just saw that it was cheaper," Clara teases.

"I'll admit, that may have been part of it," Toby grins, "but then I thought, why not? We've never had this dish as adults, so maybe it's actually good?"

"I mean," Clara pauses, tapping her fingers on the back of the wooden chair. "It's not the worst idea you've ever had."

"Why, thank you," Toby responds, setting the dish between the two place settings.

"And your timing is pretty perfect," she comments, sitting down and placing a napkin on her lap.

Toby lifts a hand and waves it in front of her face.

"What?" Clara asks, slapping it away.

"Is my sister in there?" he teases. "Two compliments in less than five minutes. Are you sick?" he asks, placing his hand to her forehead.

"Alright, alright," she says, waving him off. "Don't make me wait for this food any longer or I'm going to get a lot less complimentary."

Toby sits and allows her to dish up her portion first. "Rough day?" he asks, noticing her puffy eyes and tired expression.

"Just normal," she answers, spooning the juices out of the pan.

"What exactly do they have you working on for this internship?" he questions, reaching out for the spoon now that Clara's finished.

"Well right now I'm working with our team on this employee appreciation event coming up."

"That's part of 'Global Communications'?" Toby asks skeptically.

"Definitely," she answers, waiting as he ladles the gravy over his meat.

"I obviously don't fully understand what that title covers. I just assumed you would be communicating things about Nike to the world," he laughs, resting the spoon in the dish and noticing Clara's impatient expression. "Sorry, you could've started eating, I didn't realize you were waiting for me."

Clara rolls her eyes and picks up her fork. Toby follows suit. When the steak hits his tongue, the flavor of tomatoes and herbs fills his mouth. He looks at Clara for a reaction as she swallows her first bite.

"I think Mom might've been too hard on him," Clara says, smiling.

"Right? This is pretty good!" Toby smiles, obviously proud of his creation.

Though they are chewing in silence, Toby takes great satisfaction in noticing Clara's general excitement for her meal. He shakes his head at his still-very-present desire for approval and recognition.

"Did you call them today?" Clara asks.

"Mmm-hmm," he answers, his mouth still full.

Clara's eyebrows lift in surprise. "What'd Dad say?"

"Oh," he says, leaning back in his chair, wiping the corner of his mouth with his sleeve. "I didn't call *them*. I thought you meant the townhome rentals."

Clara stares at him. "Why would I have meant the townhome rentals?" she asks, her voice flat. "I thought we decided that was a terrible idea."

Toby hesitates, swallowing his bite. "Ummm, I didn't think we really decided anything—"

"What did you do?" Clara asks, slamming her fork to the table.

"I thought—"

"You thought? Did you rent a townhome, Toby?" she demands.

"There was one right next to—"

"Seriously?" she nearly shrieks. "Tob, you need a job first! There's no way your student loan money will last more than a few months in that neighborhood, nevermind the fact that you shouldn't even be using that money in the first place since you have no way to pay it back, and, since you're not in school, you technically should be making payments—"

"Clara, whoa! I haven't told you the best part," Toby cuts her off, placing a hand on her arm in an attempt to settle her down.

Clara stops, her eyes wary.

"I have plenty of money to cover the first six months, without breaking into the student loan money!" he says excitedly.

Clara's eyes shift and her eyebrows furrow. "Ummm—how? How is that even possible? Did you sell a kidney?"

Toby laughs, his easy chuckle contagious. "No, I sold the car!"

Nearly choking on her own spit, Clara's eyes grow wide. "You sold the—! Toby, didn't Dad pay that off, like, literally a month ago? Wasn't that a Christmas gift?"

"Totally! It's all mine now—or it was—and I realized if I sold it, I could afford the townhouse, and it's so close to the grocery store and that whole shopping area—I won't even need a car."

Toby grins from ear to ear, his excitement for his solution nearly palpable. Taking in his worn Foo Fighters t-shirt, Clara stares at him, her mouth hanging slightly open.

"What do you think?" he asks.

"I—" Clara starts, then places her hands in her lap and closes her mouth.

"Wow, okay," Toby says, lifting his plate from the table. "I thought you'd be thrilled that I'm moving out—and a week early, I never do anything early, Clar."

She sighs. "It's not that, I just don't think—"

"That this is the most responsible choice. Yep, got it," he finishes, his head hanging as he leaves the kitchen and pads down the hallway to the guest room.

WITH HIS BOXES taped up and loaded into the trunk, Toby slumps into the passenger side of Clara's Subaru. As Clara takes her seat next to him, he turns his head and looks out the window.

"Tob—" Clara starts, putting the key in the ignition. "Toby, will you at least look at me?" she petitions. "It takes at least twenty-five minutes to get to Southeast Portland from Beaverton, and it's going to be awkward if we don't even talk."

He turns, his curls bobbing.

"You need to cut your hair," she teases, but reaches out when he begins to turn away again. "I'm kidding! I actually really love your hair. I don't know how you got all the curls, when I got...this," she motions to her straightened hair, pointing out a section that has already begun to frizz in the humidity.

Slow drops of rain hit the windshield as she pulls the car out onto the street.

"I'm sorry I reacted the way I did when you told me about the townhome," Clara says apologetically.

Toby clenches his jaw.

"If I'm being honest," she continues, "I still don't think it's the most practical choice, but I guess I understand your reasoning. It *is* a walkable neighborhood. And you will save a lot by not paying for gas and insurance."

"And registration," Toby adds.

Clara grins. "And that." With her hands gripping the

steering wheel and eyes on the glassy road ahead of her, she asks, "Can you forgive me?"

Toby reaches out a hand and pats her closest shoulder. "Already done."

CHAPTER 6

Toby smooths his hair as he steps back from the door expectantly. After living here for over a week, he has yet to glimpse any of his neighbors coming or going. Yesterday, someone gained entrance to this home—the one directly next to his—first thing in the morning. A worker of some sort. He had watched as the woman had knocked and waited on the step for at least five minutes before the door was finally opened.

This morning, as he mowed his lawn in the sunshine, he couldn't help but notice the unkempt condition of the lawn next door. Feeling especially neighborly, he decided to mow it, too. Then, remembering that he shouldn't make assumptions, he figured he should probably ask permission first. "*What if you break a sprinkler head?*" he can almost hear Clara warning.

So here he stands. When the door remains shut after his first set of knocks, Toby lifts his hand and begins hammering out a jovial rhythm on the wooden surface. No amount of waiting is going to be able to kill his mood this morning. He's paying for his own home and doing his own yard work on a beautiful sunny day after almost a week of gloomy weather. With these thoughts racing through his brain, his random knocks begin to morph into a version of "Yellow Submarine" by the Beatles, so he goes with it. His hips swing subtly side to side as his toes lift on each beat, tapping on the concrete step as his head nods emphatically with the rhythm.

When the door flies open leaving his fist in midair, he is surprised so thoroughly that he nearly falls over backward and down the steps into the overgrown grass. Thankfully, his opposite hand finds the metal railing, saving him from a rather embarrassing fate in front of his new neighbor.

"Good morning!" he says cheerily, regaining his balance. Looking up, he takes in the old woman before him. The striped cat on the front of her pink sweatshirt draws his attention immediately, but then he notices her hair. White and fluffy, like clouds. Or candy floss.

Jo stares at him across the precipice.

"Do you like the Beatles?" he asks.

"Didn't you see the 'no soliciting' sign as you entered the neighborhood?" Jo asks, her voice sour.

"Ummm, no. I definitely did not. But I don't think that applies to me. Or does it?"

Jo looks at him in stunned silence. "Are you selling something?" she asks finally.

"Nope."

"Trying to get signatures for your likely terrible political agenda?"

"Nope, no clipboard here," he answers, showing her his empty hands.

"Do you want to check my roof?"

"Should I? Is it leaking?" he asks with concern, tilting his head and inspecting the shingles within his view.

"No, it's not leaking!" she snaps. "Why, exactly, are you here knocking "Yellow Submarine" on my door?"

"Ah! You know it! I hoped you'd like that one."

Jo stares at him, demanding an explanation in her steely gaze.

"Right. I'm Toby, and I just moved in next door, I wondered if I could mow your lawn—"

"My lawn is fine," Jo says, beginning to close the door.

"Wait, are you watching *Days of Our Lives*?" Toby asks, stepping closer as tense conversation carries through the door to the step.

When she doesn't shut him out immediately, he asks, "Mind if I?" and cautiously steps into the living room. "I've missed all the episodes this week since I don't have a TV yet. I completely forgot it was on right now," he shrugs and Jo, still unsure what to think of this audacious young man and his obvious ineptitude at interpreting social cues, motions him toward the sofa.

"Is it really alright if I join you?" he asks, already taking a seat, his eyes never leaving the television set.

"As long as you don't talk," Jo grunts, and Toby mimics a zipper across his lips.

Though it's distracting at first to have someone seated next to her on the couch—and he parked it right on top of her favorite quilt, mind you—Jo becomes slightly less annoyed when he mutters, "Now that's a terrible idea," before she can think it. Quite validating, actually, to hear another human agree with her. Maybe it was, in fact, worth the effort to put on pants this morning.

"Can you believe she did that?" Toby exclaims, standing and folding the blanket that had been trapped underneath him and laying it on the cushion. "The nerve! And after all Brady's done to help her," he sighs, stretching his legs to the side of the coffee table.

"Ridiculous," Jo agrees. "I mostly hate her character."

"But at least it's consistent," Toby argues, raising his eyebrows as if daring her to disagree. Slapping his hands to his legs, he says, "Well, I've got to finish the lawn, I can do yours too if you want?"

Before she can respond, Toby stands. "Oh!" he exclaims and jumps, looking down to find a fluffy Persian cat rubbing up against his leg. "And who's this?" he asks, sitting back down and placing her on his lap.

"Precious," Jo answers, surprised that the cat braved the living room with a stranger present. I guess he has been here a while, she thinks, justifying the strange behavior.

"She is absolutely precious," he coos, scratching under her chin and listening to her purr, despite her grumpy expression. "But what's her name?"

Jo laughs, the sound bursting out of her like a caged bird.

Toby glances up, taken by surprise, a grin stretching from ear to ear. "What? What's so funny?" he asks, waiting for an explanation.

Wiping a tear from her eye, Jo takes a breath. "That's her name. Precious."

"Ah," Toby laughs, his shoulders still hunched over the cat, "but you can see my confusion, right?"

Jo nods, her stomach aching slightly from the unexpected exertion. "She likes you."

"How could she not?" Toby asks, touching his nose to the cat's, and laughing when Precious attempts to lick him.

"I'll see you again next time," he promises to Precious, placing her back on the rug. "You, too, Jo!" he calls, stepping out the door and jumping down the steps. "Can I watch again with you Monday?" he calls.

"Don't you have a job?" she shouts through the open door.

"Not yet," he says, returning and poking his head in. "See you then!"

. . .

Jo, still sitting on the couch where Toby left her, stares at the clock as she strokes the cat, now occupying Toby's empty seat. Precious mews softly, reminding her that she hasn't served breakfast yet. At least, she didn't think she had. Did I eat? she questions, looking around to find evidence of her own meal. Finding nothing, she hoists herself up and follows the familiar path from the sofa to the kitchen. Precious winds through her legs as usual, eagerly awaiting her food. Once the can is opened and the dish set on the floor, Jo opens the fridge and scans the shelves, finding them surprisingly empty.

"I just went to the store last week," she frets, pulling out the last container of yogurt. It's not that going to the store is always unpleasant...well, yes, she thinks. It really is that. Walking there is difficult enough, but then all the people and the noise...Sighing, she decides she can probably last through today with this yogurt and the half empty box of crackers in the cupboard. Debating over opening a can of soup, she quickly realizes that she doesn't have a slice of bread or butter to go with it and decides to leave it on the shelf.

Resigning herself to make the dreaded trek in the morning, she carries her meager meal to the table and proceeds to inspect every inch of the kitchen. Toby seemed nice, but that's how they get you, she thinks, meticulously checking the number of faux grapes in the fruit dish. Grapes, she thinks, stepping back. I should get some of those in the morning.

CHAPTER 7

Shuffling down the sidewalk in her New Balance sneakers, Jo pushes her collapsible shopping cart ahead of her. Cheri purchased this for her before she passed, and it is exponentially more convenient than attempting to carry bags on her arms, even if the store is only three blocks. I wish I would have had a chance to tell her how much I love it, Jo thinks regretfully.

Though clouds fill the sky, rain isn't predicted until later this evening. Jo pulls her pink sweater tightly around her chest as she stops at the first crosswalk. This is just one of the many reasons why she despises going outside. It's always too cold or too hot, never exactly comfortable. Though I haven't been truly comfortable since the 80's, she thinks, scoffing at another dip in the sidewalk.

As she passes pedestrians on the street, not a single person acknowledges her; they simply move around her, as if avoiding a pothole or a speed bump. She can almost feel the annoyance from the driver behind the wheel of a grey Mercedes as she sluggishly makes her way across the third—and final—crosswalk before reaching the store.

She put on her best blue slacks and her favorite floral blouse for the trip and even took five minutes to blow dry her soft, white curls. Though, with her hair as fine and wispy as it is, a full dry only takes about one minute these days. When she had assessed herself in the mirror before leaving, she thought she had looked quite nice. Nice, ha! What do I know of nice? The fashions now are completely different from my day, and even if I knew what was 'in' these days, I certainly wouldn't be willing to put in the time and effort to participate. Her eyes linger on a woman in the parking lot, her hair tied into a nest on top of her head, her sunglasses the size of saucers. Is that 'in'? Who in their right mind would want to wear those gargantuan frames on their face? She shakes her head and continues down the sidewalk.

As the automatic doors open to Trader Joe's, she turns to the right, beginning her usual pattern through the store. Picking a bag of iceberg lettuce, she moves on to select a package of peas, and then a stir-fry kit. Turning around, she chooses a few apples from the center stands, along with a bunch of under-ripe bananas. Then, crossing the aisle, she selects a box of her favorite maple instant oatmeal. A puff of sweetness wafts from the box as she places it in the cart and she breathes it in.

Last month, her budget hadn't allowed her to purchase any extras. Somehow, her bank account hadn't matched her record on the back of her checkbook and by the last week of the month, her account had nearly been overdrawn. She furrows her brow, still perplexed as to how that would have happened when she is so meticulous about keeping financial records. In any case, no oatmeal was purchased on her last trip, but now...she grins as she catches another glimpse of it in her cart. Quite the little luxury.

Methodically, she moves through each aisle, placing her needed—and a few wanted—items in her cart. As she turns the corner, her head snaps up at the unexpected sound of her name.

"Jo!" a man's voice calls over the din of the other shoppers. Not finding the source of the sound immediately, she carefully turns her head in the opposite direction and eventually sees a mound of curly hair rapidly closing the distance between her and the deli section.

"Hey!" Toby greets her, a broad smile stretching across his boyish face. His arms and legs seem out of proportion with the rest of his body as he lopes closer. "What are you doing here?" he asks.

"Grocery shopping," she answers blandly, still in shock at the sudden interruption of her routine. What was it that she needed to get next?

"Me too, though I don't really know this store too well. What are you getting?" he asks curiously, leaning over to inspect her cart. Feeling suddenly self-conscious, she begins to walk in the direction he just appeared from.

Toby's basket swings in his arms as he follows her. "That's a good idea, I love cheese, and I noticed you before I could really take in all of their offerings," he comments, scanning the myriad options as they close in. Jo watches as he selects three different kinds of salami and a wedge of cheddar from the refrigerated display.

"Do you think this is enough for a week?" he asks.

"Enough for a few weeks, I would think," she comments.

Toby chuckles, "You don't know how much I eat," he says, then notices Jo looking him up and down. "I know, I'm skinny, but I promise I consume a lot," he assures her. "Here, I'm going to go grab a few fruits and veggies—try to be healthy and all that—but will you wait for me at the front? Then we can walk home together. It shouldn't take long!" he insists, turning without waiting for a reply.

Jo watches him take off in the opposite direction, easily

navigating the people moving through the store. Looking around, she gathers her thoughts enough to return to the previous aisle and pick up where she left off. What was it that she needed again? Sighing, she begins to scan the shelves, hoping that something will trigger her memory. Not for the first time, she finds herself wishing that she was better about keeping a grocery list.

"So do you go grocery shopping every Saturday?" Toby asks as they exit the store.

"I wait as long as humanly possible to go grocery shopping," Jo answers.

"But at least once a week?" he asks.

She shakes her head. "More like every three."

"Wow, that will last you three weeks?" he asks. "What about milk? Or fresh produce?"

"When I run out, I run out."

"So you just go without until you go to the store again? Is it too hard to walk down here more often than that?"

Jo breathes heavily as they begin the slight incline back to the house. It's not a large hill, but intense enough for Jo's worn out knees to complain almost instantly.

"It's not too hard," she answers, "I just don't like going outside of my house."

"Why?" Toby asks, still bouncing along easily beside her.

"Do you always ask so many questions?"

"I don't have to," he says, and they walk in silence for a moment. Eventually, Toby slides his bags up his arms and reaches over to take the pushcart.

"What are you doing?" Jo asks.

"It seems like you're breathing heavy so I thought I would push the cart," he explains.

"And then I'll fall on my face," Jo accuses, pulling the handle out of his grip. "I need this to keep my balance."

"Got it, sorry. Just trying to be helpful," he explains, shrugging.

When the terrain levels out, Jo gradually begins to catch her breath. "So why did you move in next door?" she asks, her face flushed.

"Because I needed a house to stay in," he answers matter-of-factly. "Actually, because I needed a place and I didn't want roommates—I've done that for too long already—and I couldn't live with my sister anymore—she thinks I'm really irresponsible—and I had to sell my car to be able to afford rent, so I needed a walkable neighborhood," he answers in a rush, walking backwards so they can talk face to face.

Jo blinks, taking a moment to process. "You're going to trip," she says, watching his feet skim the uneven surface with each blind, precarious step.

He shrugs.

"So why aren't you in school?" she continues. "Aren't you too young to be out on your own?"

"I'm twenty-one, and I think that's plenty old. I still might go back and finish my degree, but...I needed a break," he says, finally turning back around and walking beside her.

Jo relaxes. "Are your parents close by?" she asks.

"No, my dad and step-mom live in Minnesota."

"Which part?"

"St. Paul."

"And your mom?"

"She died a few years back," he answers with no hesitation.

Jo halts on the sidewalk, but it takes Toby a moment to notice. When he does, he stops and turns on his heel, cocking his head to the side.

"I'm sorry," Jo says softly. "She must have been young."

"She was," Toby nods, shoving his hands in his back pockets. "I miss her every day."

Jo lowers her eyes, then slowly begins to resume her forward motion, noticing that they are only a few lots down from her own home. That went faster than usual, she thinks.

"Jo!" an elderly voice calls from across the street, and Toby turns. Jo, however, continues walking.

"Jo, I think someone's calling you," Toby informs her, but she waves him off.

"Jo, honey, it's me. Rowena," the woman calls, putting her hand to her mouth to act as an amplifier.

Clenching her teeth, Jo turns to acknowledge her. Forcing a smile to her face, she waves. Looking both ways, Rowena places a hand on the Toyota parked along the street and steps off of the curb onto the asphalt. Cautiously, she waddles into the street toward them.

"Hold tight," Jo quips. "We may be here all day."

Toby watches with amusement as the small woman crosses the street, her Crocs moving only a few inches with each step. She looks as though she could barely weigh a hundred pounds and he half-worries that a stiff breeze will pick up and carry her off. Finally, she approaches the curb and Toby rushes to assist her, holding out a hand.

"Oh, thank you, dear. Such a nice young man," she flatters. "Is this your grandson, Jo?" she calls, louder than she needs to now that she is close.

"Rowena, you know I don't have any grandchildren who live close," Jo answers, annoyed.

"Well, they could be visiting," she counters, her voice innocent.

Jo turns, making a face, and continues to push the cart toward her townhome.

"Jo, my goodness, you are spry. Let me catch up," Rowena says, leaving Toby's side and following behind her.

Jo stops and turns to her. "What do you need? I have groceries I need to unload," she says impatiently.

"Oh, honey, I don't need anything," Rowena says, finally arriving next to her and tottering to a halt. Her glasses slip to the end of her nose, but she doesn't bother to adjust them. "I've been meaning to catch you. A few of us are starting a Bunco group and thought perhaps you'd like to join," she offers sweetly. "Sunday afternoons."

"Why Sunday?" Jo asks, resting a hand on her hip.

"Because...that seemed like a nice time to do it," Rowena smiles.

"But we aren't doing anything any other day of the week, so why wait 'til the weekend?"

"Well, I have my hair appointments on Tuesdays and Roy—"

"Roy's coming?" Jo frowns, cutting her off.

"Of course," Rowena laughs, reaching into her sweater pocket for a tissue. "Wouldn't be a party without Roy."

"Uh-huh, well count me out," Jo mutters, turning away and starting up the walkway toward her steps.

Rowena watches in confusion as Jo attempts to storm away, her hands twisting around the tissue anxiously. Toby sets his own groceries on the sidewalk and follows Jo, nodding at Rowena as he passes.

"So who are you, then?" she asks.

"Me?" Toby says, turning back to face her. "I just moved in," he explains, pointing next door.

"Oh!" Rowena exclaims, placing a hand on her heart. "Well I had no idea we had a new neighbor," she says excitedly. "You know, you are more than welcome to attend our Bunco game. It's really not exclusive at all," she says, winking. "The more the merrier."

Toby grins. "Well thanks," he says. "It's at your place?"

Rowena points across the street. "Blue house with the white curtains. I always make sweet tea."

"I'll let you know if I can make it," Toby promises, then hastily turns to help Jo with her bags.

"Just open the door, I'll take them into the kitchen for you," he offers, slinging the handles over his arms. Surprisingly, she accepts his help without a fight.

After setting the bags down in the kitchen, he heads back to the walk, folds her cart, and effortlessly lifts it inside, stowing it next to the coat rack while Jo watches from the entryway.

"Sorry, not sure if that's where it lives," he admits. "I would help you put away the groceries, but I don't know where anything goes. My sister hates it when I put stuff in the wrong spot."

"There aren't any wrong spots, just better ones," Jo says.

Toby smiles, rocking slightly on his feet. "Why don't you want to go to Bunco?" he asks awkwardly. Rolling her eyes, Jo makes her way to the couch and sits, leaning down to remove her shoes.

"Rowena seems nice," he continues, gauging her reaction.

"Oh she is nice," Jo responds sarcastically. "They're all nice. And completely void of anything interesting or meaningful."

"How so?" Toby asks, intrigued at her assessment.

"All they care about is who's dating who, and whose grandchild is doing what, and where they're planning to cruise to next. I think I'm actually becoming more vain and substance-less just by thinking about it."

Unable to help himself, Toby laughs out loud. "Jo, seriously? They can't be that bad."

"You go to Bunco and then let me know what you think," she challenges, pulling her quilt to her lap.

"Well maybe I will. Maybe I love Bunco."

"Have you ever played before?" she asks.

"That's beside the point," Toby hedges, laughing.

"That's what I thought," Jo says finally, flicking on the TV.

Grinning, Toby motions to the kitchen. "I'm going to put your cold stuff in the fridge," he informs her and she waves him off. "Anything else you need?"

"I could use some help putting away some of my bowls. I'm not tall enough to reach the top cupboards, and using a step stool seems like a recipe for a broken hip," she calls.

"Sure!" he agrees, and takes in the cluttered kitchen counters. "*Some* bowls, Jo?" he teases. "What have you been doing in here?"

Jo reluctantly leaves her comfortable spot and joins him in the kitchen. Ignoring his comment, she gives instructions on which dish goes where. Within minutes, the counters are clear again.

"How did you possibly use that many bowls?" Toby asks again, pulling his shirt back down after placing the last one in the tallest cupboard.

"They've been collecting for a year or so," Jo admits.

"A year?" Toby exclaims. "Wow, you're even lazier than I am," he teases, gently nudging her shoulder on his way past. "Gotta get my own milk in the fridge. See you for *Days*?"

Again, not waiting for a reply, he rushes out the front door, closing it behind him. Nice young man, Jo thinks. Ugh. I sound like Rowena. Disgusted with herself, she pulls out a glass from the cupboard and fills it with water. Then she counts her grapes.

CHAPTER 8

As Sunday afternoon rolls around, Toby watches out the front window. He had failed to ask for an exact time on the Bunco game and, rather than walk across the street and ask, he is instead watching for when people will begin arriving at the house. Nothing yet. Striding into the kitchen, he opens the refrigerator in search of a snack. Snacks, he thinks, his eyes widening. Should he take snacks over when he goes to Rowena's?

Shutting the door, he opens the cupboard and scans for an easy option. Trail mix. Perfect, he smiles, pulling the bag from the shelf. With that disaster averted, he returns to the fridge and pulls a frozen burrito from the freezer. He wraps it in a paper towel after ripping open the plastic and sets it on a plate in the microwave. Pressing 'start', he glances out the front window to see an elderly man walking up the steps to Rowena's door, with another woman holding a cane a few steps behind.

Toby pulls the burrito out and quickly scarfs it down—somehow burning his tongue while also finding a bite that is still frozen as he eats. Snatching the trail mix from the counter, he leaves the house and jogs across the street.

THIS TIME, the door opens almost instantaneously after he knocks, and Rowena's face lights up when she sees him.

"Oh, well! I'm so glad you made it!" she greets him, her expression warm and grandmotherly. "Remind me of your name again, honey."

"It's Toby," he answers, stepping into the living room, the scent of floral perfume nearly bowling him over.

"Everyone, this is Toby," Rowena announces. "He just moved in across the street."

Wrinkled, smiling faces greet him from a trio of card tables set up in the center of the room. Rowena's home seems to be double the size of his, or at least the living room must be. Toby doubts he could set up three tables in his front room without having them hit both side walls and smack up against each other.

A man with combed white hair motions to Toby and he walks closer. "Us fellas have to stick together," the man says, motioning for him to sit. "I'm Roy," he continues, offering his hand as Toby obediently pulls out the chair next to him.

Shaking it, Toby sits. "Nice to meet you," he says. "It's helpful to put a face to a name."

"Oh? My reputation precedes me?" he comments cheekily, pulling a cigar from his breast pocket.

"No smoking in here, Roy!" a woman commands from the next table over. He waves her off and lights up anyway.

"I wouldn't say 'reputation', but I have heard your name. Jo and Rowena—"

"Ah, those two can't get enough of me," he laughs, leaning back in his chair. Toby can't help but be impressed with his confidence. His shirt is unbuttoned just enough for silver chest hair to be visible, standing out against his tanned skin. Jo did mention cruising, and this guy almost certainly didn't build that skin color in drizzly Oregon.

"Don't listen to a thing he says," a silver-haired woman says, leaning over and placing a bony hand on Toby's shoulder. "He's all smoke and mirrors."

"Especially smoke," another woman grouses, but Roy simply smiles, revealing creases in the leathery skin around his mouth and eyes. He motions for Toby to come closer.

"They're all jealous because I've got a new girlfriend," he informs him. "She's sixty-two and these broads can't stand it."

Just then, Rowena re-enters the room with a rolling tray stacked with cookies and a pitcher of sweet tea.

"And this is why I come, right there," Roy whispers. "Her Russian wedding cookies are to die for."

Toby inspects the cart, attempting to figure out which cookies Roy could be referring to, but none of them look particularly familiar. Rowena rolls the cart to him first, and he gratefully picks up a paper plate.

"Try one of each, honey," she insists, and Toby is happy to oblige.

"Do I get to try one of each?" Roy asks flirtatiously when Toby has finished.

"Maybe if you put that cigar out," Rowena complains, waving her hand in front of her face dramatically.

Sighing, Roy uses a paper plate to stamp it out, then picks up a new one for his cookies. Rowena takes the cart around the room and Toby begins sampling the cookies on his plate. First, he tries one that looks like a double-decker, stuck together with some sort of jam. With dainty frills around the edges and a heart cut out of the center, it seems almost too beautiful to eat. Somehow, Toby manages.

A woman passes a scorecard and pencil to Toby.

"I've actually never played before," he admits.

"I'm sure you'll catch on no problem," she assures him.

"You basically just roll the dice and hope to get the same number as round," Roy explains. "You want ones in this first round." Toby nods.

"You and me," the plump woman across from him states. "Let's take these two down," she says, winking and rolling up the sleeves of her cardigan. Toby suppresses a laugh.

As the round starts, Toby does exactly as he's told but, while the game is fairly entertaining, he is far more interested in the conversation around him.

"Did you hear," the woman next to him starts, "that Sheila's son got a girl pregnant?"

"No!" his teammate gasps. "What girl. The one he was dating or that loose gal that is always over at their house?"

"Oh, well, I guess I didn't think to ask," the first woman admits.

"Probably both," Roy jumps in, but the women don't even miss a beat.

"And I heard that Terry had an affair."

"No! Lenora's son?"

As Toby switches tables round after round, the gossip continues to fly. Far more dramatic than any soap opera, he continually wonders how Jo didn't find this entertaining, considering her love of *Days*. The sheer breadth of information is mind-boggling. Are all of these people still living in the area, he wonders? Is that how these women know so much about their lives? Or is there some sort of grandparent informational hotline that he isn't aware of? How many people right now are hearing, *"Did you hear that Clarke's son dropped out of Madison?"* Toby shudders at the thought.

"You did well," Roy says, clapping him on the back.

"It's really just luck," Toby comments, looking at his win-loss record. "But at least I figured out how to play."

Roy laughs, slipping into a pair of Sperry Topsiders. "It was good to have some young blood here, Rowena," he calls, opening the door and tipping his hat to the women in the room. "And glad I wasn't the only dapper gentlemen in attendance this time." He winks at Toby and strides down the steps, allowing the door to close behind him.

CHAPTER 9

On Friday, Toby sits on Jo's couch as the last *Days of Our Lives* episode for the week finishes and the theme music begins to play. His plans earlier in the week to watch were thwarted when he lined up job interviews. Turns out, businesses like to conduct those during regular hours.

"What did you think?" he asks, still staring at the screen.

"That woman's got something up her sleeve," Jo declares.

"Agreed. I just don't know what it is. Do you think she's going to try to kill him?"

"Huh," Jo responds, leaning back on the sofa. "I never considered that."

Toby turns and a goofy smile spreads across his face. "You know, I have to tell you. You have great skin, Jo. Every time I see you, I can't believe how smooth it looks. It's kind of like you are always in front of one of those old movie lenses—you know the ones where they put vaseline on the glass to make the image look soft? Especially after looking at all of those faces on Sunday—"

Jo stares at him, unblinking, adjusting her glasses on her nose. "Sunday?" she asks.

"Yeah, at Bunco," Toby reminds her, and she bursts out laughing.

"You actually went?"

"Hey, you told me to," he retorts. "It was actually pretty fun, too, I don't know why you're so against it."

Jo wipes her eyes, "I bet you got an earful."

"I definitely did," he agrees, "but it was like a real-life soap opera. I couldn't figure out why you were so opposed to it when it was so entertaining."

"You found that entertaining?" she asks meaningfully.

Toby hesitates. "In the sense that it was dramatic and over the top, sure," he justifies.

Jo sniffs. "Well good for you."

"Jo, I think it's pretty harmless—"

"Harmless? Maybe so, until it's you that they're talking about," she huffs, folding her arms and turning the other direction.

"Is that what happened?" Toby asks sincerely. "Did they talk about you?"

Jo is silent. Eventually she pushes herself upright and walks to the kitchen. Toby follows.

"Of course they talked about me," she murmurs. "How could they not? I'm not like them. I didn't raise my kids here, or start a local business, or donate to a scholarship fund. I'm not like them. And they know it."

"But they still invite you—"

"Ha!" Jo interjects. "They invite because they want to feel good about themselves, not because they actually hope I'll come."

Toby nods watching Jo search in the silverware drawer for something. "I'm sorry, Jo. I didn't realize—"

"I think the workers from Simply Living are stealing from me," Jo blurts out. Toby steps back, his eyes widening. She realizes it probably wasn't the best transition, but she just couldn't hold it in any longer. Searching in the drawer reminded her of the missing serving spoon and, with her emotions already running high, it just bubbled out.

"What?" he asks, incredulous. "What did they steal?" he asks, stroking Precious, who decided to leave her spot on the couch to wind around their ankles, clearly hoping for extra food.

"My porcelain bell," she says, pointing to the end table by the couch. "It used to sit right there. And an apple from my fruit basket."

"Like a real apple?" he asks.

"No, from my decorative basket over there," she points to the table next to them. "I think they're also stealing money."

Toby lets out a low whistle. "How? Like from your wallet?"

She nods. "Sometimes. They give me cash each week for my expenses, but some weeks it's less than others. They say it's the same, but I know it's not. I've been keeping track." She reaches under a magazine on the coffee table and pulls out a notepad. A running column of numbers stretches down the page and, Toby notices, they are significantly different in some instances.

"Huh," he says. "That's not cool. Have you reported it? And why are they in charge of your money in the first place?"

"Something my daughter set up before she died, which," she waggles her finger, "If I ever get the chance to discuss *that* with her, let me tell you. I can only assume she thought it would be helpful for me, she couldn't have known..." she trails off, then suddenly remembers her thought. "And I have reported it, but," she pauses, "they aren't taking it seriously. They say they've looked into it and there isn't any evidence. They've gone as far as accusing me of misplacing things."

"Why would you do that?"

"Exactly."

"Do you have the same worker every time?"

"No, it's different. I think it's the man who stole the bell, but the woman I reported it to said 'why would a thirty year old man want a bell?'," she quotes, flipping her hair and doing her best to impersonate a dumb blonde.

Toby leans forward and laughs out loud, causing Precious to startle and scurry to the bedroom. "Do that again, please," he begs, but Jo waves him off. When he catches his breath, he reiterates, "So no one believes you?"

"They say they do, but then nothing is actually done about it."

"Well, then *we* need to do something about it," Toby says, slapping his hands down on the counter. The sound is louder than he anticipated and it causes both of them to jump. "But," he continues, "there *is* a slight problem."

"What's that?" Jo asks.

"I just got a job."

Jo's eyes widen in surprise.

"I know, I'm as disappointed as you that I won't be able to watch *Days* all next week like we planned, but I think I can still catch it twice. That's better than I did this week, honestly. I'm going to be working at Bob's, the Italian place down the street!" he announces triumphantly.

"Are they going to make you cut your hair?" she asks.

"They didn't say anything about it," he says, "so I'm assuming no?"

"You're going to be a waiter?"

"Yep, I start training Monday."

Jo nods.

"So, we'll need to plan when I'm not working. I don't really know what my full schedule will be yet. I'll think about potential options tonight and then when I get my shifts, we can put something together—tomorrow if that works? I already know my training schedule. Want to come to my house for lunch? We could have cheese and salami," he suggests, pausing slightly, waiting for a response. When she doesn't immediately say 'no', he waves and walks out the door with a grin on his face.

She returns to the couch—not quite sure why she didn't refuse his offer—and flicks open the blinds to watch him walk down the sidewalk.

Across the street, her attention is drawn to Roy, strutting down the street with that—that hussy again. Where does he find these women? They all have to be at least twenty years younger than him. She watches Roy wave to Toby, showing off his prize. Look at her, primping next to him, her falsies nearly up to her neck with her little Pomeranian trotting at the end of an abrasively fluorescent pink leash.

"Ugh!" she grunts, pulling her finger back and allowing the blind to snap into place as she plops on the couch cushion. Glancing up at the wall, her eyes land just below the swishing tail of the clock on the last picture taken of Walter. His face beams back at her, his fishing pole just visible in the space behind his right ear. Did Cheri take this? Did I? Though it's been ten years, she can still imagine him telling her to 'stop bothering with the neighbors and just worry about yourself'. He was always so good about reminding her to stop wasting time on things that didn't matter.

She tried once—to join him. Swallowed a whole bottle of pain pills a year or so ago, but it only made her sick. When she woke up in the hospital, they told her she wouldn't be able to keep medications anymore, at least not that many. The aides bring her a few replacements every now and then when she needs to use them, but her Medicaid card won't allow her to purchase anything from the drugstore. Well, that's not completely true. She can buy bandaids and wart remover, but what good is that? Unable to think of another painless way to end it, she had resigned herself to slogging through.

A few days later, Precious ended up on her porch. With no collar and her ribs visible through her dirty, matted fur, Jo took her in. Now, she figures she needs to at least stick around for her.

As if sensing her thoughts, Precious meows in the kitchen. Dinner already? Jo forces herself upright and walks into the kitchen, accidentally kicking a grocery bag on the floor. She stares at it. Didn't I already put everything away? Looking inside, she laughs to herself. So that's where that was, she thinks, picking up the box of oatmeal. She had been searching for that and thought it had been left at the store, or had somehow fallen out during her visit from Rowena. It had been easy to blame her for mishap. Slowly, she organizes the forgotten items, stacking them in various cupboards, and rolls up the bag under the sink. Another complaint from Precious reminds her to pull a can of cat food from the shelf.

"Alright, alright," she answers, pulling on the tab opener of one of the newer cans and reaching for a clean bowl. The cat purrs, moving in a figure eight around her ankles. "What would you do without me?" Jo coos, then places the food on the floor.

CHAPTER 10

"You again?" Jo asks, disappointed at seeing a man in a crisp white shirt—the Simply Living logo on his chest—standing on her step with an umbrella. She had rushed to the door in the hopes that Toby hadn't gone to work yet. Instead, she finds herself face to face with the suspected thief.

"I don't want you in my house," she spits vehemently, attempting to close the door.

"Jo, I don't know why you think that—" he starts, his voice calm.

"I don't *think, I know*. Why won't you admit you took it?" she asks, her eyes indignant. The cold, wet air rushes past her ankles causing her to shiver, but she holds the door slightly ajar to hear the man's response.

The man sighs. "Jo, I'm just trying to do my job. I need to come in and complete my assessment. Then I'll leave, I promise. And I didn't take your bell, I don't even know what it looks like—"

"Ha! That's a lie if I ever heard one. You're not coming in here," she insists, blocking his entry with her body.

"If you don't let me in, someone else will have to come by either today or tomorrow. It's up to you."

"You're not coming in," Jo maintains, slamming the door in his face. The nerve! She locks the door, huffing and placing her hands on her hips. Stomping to the window, she flicks open the blind and watches him take a few notes on his tablet, holding the umbrella between his neck and shoulder.

Closing the blinds, she lies back down on the couch and pulls the quilt up to her chin. Her heart pounds. Walter always knew what to do in situations like this. When Cheri was little, she had a propensity for thievery. Her preferred contraband? Gum from the corner store. When doing laundry, Jo would find wrappers in her pocket and, upon further investigation, she would find a new pack hidden consistently in her underwear drawer. She was only six and already Jo felt out of her element. Walter would simply chuckle when she filled him in, then follow up by gently calling Cheri into the kitchen.

"Hey honey," he would start, and Cheri would inevitably climb into his lap, wrapping her small arms around his neck. "How was your day?" he would ask and she would proceed to tell him everything. All the feelings that Jo wished she would share with her, Cheri would freely spill to Walter. Jo would sit at the table and listen, wishing she could find a way to build a relationship like that with her only daughter. So safe and free. It seemed that anything she did only drove Cheri further from her. And if she wasn't able to figure it out when the girl was six...

"Mom tells me that you took home another pack of gum from the store," Walter would say, and Cheri's eyes would lower.

"But Daddy, it was a new flavor and Mom said I didn't have any money."

"So when we don't have money, it gives us the right to take what we want?"

"Sometimes...maybe?" she would ask, innocent and unsure despite the fact that this was the third conversation of the same kind over the last few weeks.

Walter would grin and continue watching her, his eyes twinkling.

"No, Daddy. We shouldn't take things," Cheri would eventually conclude. Then Walter would lift her up and walk her to the front door where they would both put on their shoes. He would grip her tiny hand in his, and they would walk to the store and make it right. Sometimes they would come home an hour or so later, so that Cheri could work off her debt. Other times, she would work it off doing chores at home, but always it was dealt with kindly and without conflict.

Jo would watch, frustrated that the behavior continued to happen, but Walter never got angry. How was he able to stay calm? To always be the good guy even when being the disciplinarian? Cheri's pilfering only lasted a few months, thankfully, and then she either learned or grew out of it. It simply stopped happening, and Jo couldn't have been more thrilled.

She wonders how Walter would deal with this one. He definitely wouldn't have been rude, as she just was. Would he pop this Simply Living worker on his lap and look at him until he confessed? She chuckles at the mental image, then closes her eyes, allowing the audience cheers on the TV to fade into the background.

CHAPTER 11

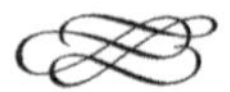

"For two," Clara says, approaching the hostess station at Bob's.

"Is your brother working?" Ian asks, scanning the dining room.

"I'm pretty sure he said he was working the dinner shift tonight. I didn't want to ask again—I wanted it to be a surprise."

As the hostess collects the menus and motions for them to follow, Clara catches her attention. "Hey, would it be possible to sit in Toby's section?"

She nods, flicking her long dark hair over her shoulder, and takes them to the patio.

"Are we okay sitting outside?" Ian whispers.

"I think so," Clara responds, following obediently. Thankfully, they are placed at a table directly next to a gas heater. "Could you turn this on for us?" Clara asks and the young hostess nods before spinning and retreating back into the restaurant. One other couple is seated on the patio, deep in conversation at the other end, but otherwise, they seem to have the section to themselves.

"Is he only working the patio?" Ian asks, beginning to scan the menu.

"You keep asking these questions, as if I somehow know more than you do," Clara teases.

"What!?" she hears Toby exclaim as the doors to the dining room swing open. "I didn't know you guys were coming tonight!" he says, obviously thrilled.

"I wanted to surprise you," Clara laughs.

"Ian, nice to see you again," Toby says politely, looking very dapper in his black slacks, pressed white shirt, and bowtie.

"You sure clean up nice," Clara comments, but then raises her eyebrow, taking in his hair. "You don't have to pull that back or something?"

"Nope, since I'm not cooking, I'm good to go," he explains proudly.

"Well, if I find a hair in my food…"

"You're being discriminatory, Clara," Toby accuses. "Look at all the female waiters with long, flowing hair," he says, pointing through the window.

"He's right," Ian agrees.

"Fine, I'm sorry. Can you turn on this heater for us?" Clara asks impatiently. "We asked the hostess, but she went back inside and we haven't seen her since."

"Yeah, I don't know how much English she speaks to be honest," he admits and Clara looks puzzled.

"How is she working here, then?" she asks.

"I don't know, I think she got the job through a friend or something," Toby answers. "I can try to turn this on, but I honestly haven't had to do this yet." He crouches down and inspects the mechanism. "It seems simple enough, as long as I don't let out too much gas and blow us up or something," he laughs nervously.

"I doubt that's possible," Ian comments off-handedly, still searching the menu.

Clara watches as Toby hits the starter, then jumps when the tube fills with flame.

"Uhhh, I'm pretty sure it's not supposed to do that," he says under his breath, jumping backward. "I think someone left the gas on." Toby glances inside to make sure nobody witnessed the mishap.

"Well it didn't blow up and it feels marvelous," Clara says, turning back to the table.

"It probably has a safety mechanism to avoid a true explosion," Ian hypothesizes.

Toby smiles nervously, his finger tapping his notepad. "Can I bring you something to drink?"

"Just waters," Clara instructs.

"I'll bring some bread, too. Shouldn't take long," Toby says, walking back inside.

Looking over the options, Clara narrows her potential choices down to two. Traditionally, she leans toward a classic chicken caesar, but the salmon looks inviting today, as well.

"What are you getting?" she asks Ian.

"Not sure yet," he says seriously. "Debating between the bolognese and the chicken marsala."

"Mmm, both sound good," Clara responds, only somewhat disappointed that he wasn't considering one of her choices so they could share.

A moment later, Toby returns with a white napkin-lined basket full of warm, seasoned ciabatta. Setting it on the table, he stands up tall, looking pleased with himself.

"Do you know what you'd like?" Toby asks, avoiding looking at Ian directly. Clara notices his avoidance and frowns. They've been dating for months now, and yes, while she understands that Toby hasn't been here for all of that, she expected they would at least be amiable at this point.

"I'd like some oil and vinegar for the bread," Ian states abruptly, and Clara purses her lips. That sort of comment isn't helping.

"I can definitely get that for you," Toby answers blandly, turning toward the patio wait station.

"We can order first," Ian suggests, stopping him. "I think I'd like the bolognese," he says, looking up from his menu. "Is it good here?"

Toby turns toward him. "I mean...I think so. But I've only worked here a week," he says truthfully.

"I'll have the chicken caesar," Clara says quickly, handing him the menu.

"Perfect, I'll go put that in for you," he offers, taking the menus and retreating again through the glass doors.

"So," Ian starts before she can say anything, "you said he dropped out of school?"

Clara sighs and nods. "He could potentially go back, but he doesn't seem very motivated at this point."

"What's his plan?" Ian asks, removing his cutlery from the white folded napkin and laying the fabric across his lap.

"I honestly don't think he has one. He's living in a townhome a few blocks up. It's way too expensive for him, but he sold his car and seems to think that money will hold him over for a while—"

Clara pauses as Toby returns, setting the glass bottles on the table, and then retreats again to the main dining room.

"Huh. Millennials, right? They somehow think they have the luxury of doing what they want all the time," Ian comments. "We'd all love to just 'do what we want' but that's not the way the world works," he says, pouring the oil and vinegar onto a small plate and breaking off a piece of bread.

"I know, I don't get it. I've tried to talk to him about it, but at this point...I don't think he's willing to listen. He's going to have to figure it out on his own. Speaking of which," she transitions, "could you do me a favor? And this has nothing to do with you or the way you're approaching things, more that I know Toby doesn't respond well to—"

"You want me to baby him, Clar?" Ian interrupts. "It sounds like he's already getting too much of that."

"Not baby him, just...make an effort to notice the good things."

Ian grunts. "For you," he says, taking a bite, "I'll try. It's nice of you to support him like this," Ian says around a mouth full of bread.

"Well I had to see where he finally got a job," she laughs gratefully. "Him choosing to work at all was not necessarily a given." She dips a piece of bread and places it in her mouth. "Hey, not bad," she says, grinning.

"It's pretty hard to mess up bread," Ian says, then dips another piece.

AFTER CLEARING THEIR PLATES, Toby returns to the computer to print their check. It feels odd asking his sister to pay for something, but he reminds himself that she chose to come in of her own volition. Placing the tab inside a black folder, he grabs a pen and moves back to the patio. As he approaches the table, Ian reaches out and takes the check from him, pulling out his wallet simultaneously in one systematic move.

"You don't have to pay," Clara offers, but Ian holds up a hand.

"Thanks so much for coming," Toby says sincerely. "I think I'm getting better, and I really enjoy talking to people."

Clara nods, smiling. "Are you getting enough shifts?"

Her thinly veiled attempt at assessing whether he can make enough money here puts Toby immediately on the defensive. He takes a deep breath before responding.

"I should be. I've put my name on the list to take extra shifts as needed, so hopefully that will fill out the week. I know a lot of people like to have the weekend off, and it's not like I have anything better to do. I'd honestly rather work in the evening anyway. Tips are better, and then it doesn't conflict with things I'd like to do during the day."

Clara looks at him, amused. "Like what?"

Ian finishes arranging the cash ostentatiously in the bill fold and hands it back to Toby, who takes it gratefully.

"Like mowing the lawn—"

"You have a lawn mower? Don't townhomes come with groundskeeping?" Ian asks, skeptical.

"The HOA does our trash and maintenance past the sidewalk, but we're responsible for our little yard in front of the house. It only takes a few minutes. I have one of those manual, push mowers. Got it free off of Craigslist," Toby explains proudly.

"Huh," Ian muses.

"Then I do my grocery shopping, hang out with Jo—she's my eighty-seven year old neighbor—he explains to Ian, flashing a look to Clara who nearly chokes on her water."

"What do you mean by 'hang out'?" Clara asks, wiping her mouth on her napkin.

"We watch *Days of Our Lives* together—"

"She lets you into her apartment?" Clara exclaims.

"Why not?" Toby asks.

"I don't know, just seems like she barely knows you—"

"I'm a pretty nice guy," he counters, flashing her a cheesy smile.

"Well, you've probably got other tables to get to," Ian announces, standing abruptly. "You ready, Clara?"

"Sure," she says hesitantly, pulling her purse from the back of the chair and rising to her feet. "Thanks for the great dinner, Toby. You did really well," she says sincerely, fiddling with her purse and following Ian through the gate to the street.

Toby waves, thanking them, and then rushes to check on the food for table nine.

CHAPTER 12

"He came by the house again?" Toby asks, incredulous.

Jo nods, taking a bite of noodles. "I didn't let him in. Thanks for the Chinese, haven't had this in ages," she says, a noodle still hanging out of the side of her mouth.

"Hopefully it won't give you indigestion," he says, awkwardly bringing the chopsticks to his mouth. He sits cross-legged on the floor with his take-out container on the coffee table. Jo didn't want to miss Jeopardy, and sitting on the couch puts too much distance between his mouth and the container.

"It doesn't really matter what I eat these days," Jo sighs, then suddenly sits up straight, jolting her take-out container, and shouts, "Infrared!" at the television screen.

Toby laughs when the answer is proven correct. "You know your stuff," he comments as Precious lifts herself to inspect his dinner, her front paws daintily placed on the edge of the table. He watches her as she sniffs the noodles.

"Living for almost nine decades will do that," she quips, sweeping the cat's paws off the furniture. Toby finds a small piece of chicken and slips it to her on the floor. She inhales it gratefully, purring.

WHEN THE PROGRAM ENDS, Toby clears their trash. He places their containers back in the paper bag and sets it by the door, knowing it won't all fit in Jo's can. When Jo returns from the bathroom, she settles back into her spot on the couch.

"Are you okay?" Toby asks, lacing his shoes.

"Just my regular," she says, waving him off. Having noticed her frequent trips to the bathroom after eating, Toby had asked if she needed to see a doctor. After enduring her annoyed gaze, he eventually learned that vomiting after meals was a normal experience for Jo. She promised that it wasn't much—definitely not an eating disorder—but he still feels a responsibility to monitor the situation closely.

Standing up to his full height, he adjusts his shirt. "So, after your interaction, that guy definitely won't be by anymore, right? Hopefully no more missing things?"

Jo purses her lips.

"Or not?" Toby asks, furrowing his brows at her expression.

Hesitating, Jo lowers her eyes. Toby waits patiently, recognizing that she tends to shut down a little whenever something makes her uncomfortable. Eventually, Jo meets his eyes, her white hair glowing like a halo from the glare of the tv.

"He's the only one who ever showed me my statements," she admits nervously.

Toby squints through his glasses. "What kind of statements. Like rent?"

"My family trust," Jo says blandly.

"Huh, you have one of those? That's cool," Toby comments, nodding his head.

"That's where I get my money every month."

"Nice."

"Not nice if it runs out before I die."

"Huh," Toby breathes. "Do you think that might happen?"

"Well I'm not planning to die tomorrow."

Toby shoves his hands in his pockets. "So how much is left in there? How long do you get to live?" he laughs, then inspects her face to make sure he didn't overstep.

"I haven't seen a statement in months," Jo answers, not missing a beat. "Usually he printed them out for me. I don't know where he got them."

"It's probably just online, don't you think? What bank are you with?"

Jo looks puzzled.

"Do you even have internet here?" Toby asks, looking around, not seeing an obvious computer monitor.

"I have no use for any of that," Jo mutters.

Toby looks at her and pushes his frames up the bridge of his nose.

"That's probably true," he chuckles. "I can help you find your statements, if you want. I would just need to know the bank and your account number."

"What, so you can steal my money, too?" Jo accuses neurotically.

Though he figures she's likely kidding, Toby says, "Nah, I don't have use for any of that," waving her off. A small smile creeps to Jo's lips.

"I'll ask the next overly invested aide when they stop by. I'm sure it won't be long since I chased the other guy away," she says, readjusting her weight on the cushion and looking slightly chagrined.

"Just let me know," Toby offers, opening the door. "I'm working the next few days, but I'll be over to mow your grass before the weekend."

"Do you like your job?" Jo calls before he moves down the steps. Realizing that this is quite possibly the first question she's ever asked regarding his personal preferences, Toby leans in.

"There are pros and cons," he admits, "but overall, I think so."

"Is it something you want to do forever?" Jo asks, still facing the tv.

"It's probably a little early to tell," he laughs. "Do you think I should?" he asks, plastering a grin on his face and waiting for the inevitable suggestion that it 'isn't a responsible choice' or 'won't provide for a family', or any other response reiterating how far he's fallen below his potential.

"Seems like a good option," she muses, "but you probably have so many things you *could* do. Must be hard to choose."

Toby blinks, not sure how to reply. "Thanks, Jo."

"For what?" she retorts as Precious jumps to her lap.

Toby allows the door to close softly, then stands on the step, taking a moment to stare at the evening sky. Though not many stars are visible, he fixes his gaze on one in particular. Breathing deeply, he watches it flicker as the breeze whispers along his cheek.

Could he do anything? His mind flashes back to his mom's face. *"You can be anything you want,"* he hears her say. Anything. The idea is so broad that it's overwhelming. What does it even mean? Sure, I could do anything, but it's not like I have the option of trying everything out and *then* deciding what would be best. I basically have to guess and hope I like it—especially if there's any sort of education involved. By the time I finish the necessary requirements, there isn't time to suddenly decide I chose wrong and start over. Have I ever even considered what I *do* want? I keep running from things I don't...but is there anything that feels right?

A familiar dull panic sits in his stomach. What if there's

nothing? What if I don't find a good fit...ever? Isn't it completely possible that I'll take to long to figure this out and my time will run out? What if all I have to look forward to is more of what I hate?

Taking another deep breath to ease the tightness in his chest, Toby slowly descends to the walkway. Doing something he hates simply doesn't feel like a viable option.

CHAPTER 13

"Toby?" Clara calls. "You in here?"

"Hey," he answers hurriedly, buttoning his pants as he walks down the hall. "Sorry, I was just in the bathroom."

"Then why is your front door unlocked?" Clara asks, raising an eyebrow.

"I definitely have a lot of cool stuff in here, just ripe for the taking," Toby answers, glancing around the bare living room.

Clara rolls her eyes and hoists a paper bag onto his kitchen counter. "I was cleaning out my stuff and thought you might want some of this," she explains, pulling out a few boxes of cereal, crackers, and cookies and setting them on the counter.

"Is it all expired or something?" he teases.

"No, I'm just trying to eat healthier."

"Cool. I'm not," he laughs.

"Well, look at you. Your metabolism is obviously still in high gear," she comments, folding the empty bag and tucking it under her arm.

"I am about to go mow Jo's lawn, do you want to come say hi?" he asks, tucking his curls behind his ears.

"No, I've got to get going," she hedges.

"I'm sure she'd be open to it, I mean, since I'm there, so she'll know you're safe," he teases.

Clara smacks his arm. "I still can't believe you're spending so much time with her. Do you not have any desire to make friends your own age?"

"I do have friends my own age," he retorts. "I spend time with some of the other servers and kitchen guys at Bob's."

"While you're working?" she asks skeptically.

"I'm working a lot, so I think that counts."

Clara sighs, retreating to the door.

"I got a job, Clar. I have my own place. What more do you want from me?" he asks, defeated, his hands hanging limply at his sides.

"I just—" she starts, but then turns to the door, thinking better of it. "Nothing, nevermind. I'm so glad things are going well for you," she says, opening the door. Rays of sunlight illuminate a triangle on the wooden entry floor, making it glow. "See you Sunday for dinner? My place?"

"Is Ian coming?" he asks, still moping slightly.

"Not sure. I think he's trying to finish up a project," she answers, turning to meet his eyes.

"Cool. Yeah, I'll try."

"You'll try?" she says, judgment in her eyes.

He nods, then gives her a small wave as she closes the door. Unmoving, he watches through the window until she drives away, then slips on his shoes and exits out the back to retrieve the mower from under the metal staircase.

AFTER SHOWERING—HIS skin was itching from the few particles of grass that made it up under his pant leg—Toby notices his phone lighting up. Recognizing the number, he closes his eyes, readying himself. Though he knew this moment would have to come sooner or later...later would've been ideal.

"Hey, Dad," he says cheerily, answering the call.

"Toby?"

"That's me," he comments, his voice already tight.

"Toby, we got a letter in the mail from Madison. Something about you needing to defer your status or risk losing your admittance there? Did you forget to register for classes this semester or something? I told you, you need to make sure and do that before—"

"Dad," he interrupts, "I'm actually not attending this semester."

The silence stretches, and Toby begins to sweat.

"What do you mean by 'not attending'?" he asks, his voice low.

"Dad, I'm just taking a break," he explains.

"A break to do what?"

"I don't know. Figure out what I want to do."

"You mean party? That's all there is to do at that school if you aren't engaged in coursework—"

"Dad, stop. Please. I'm not partying. I moved out here to Portland with Clara—"

"What? You're living with Clara?" he asks in surprise, a hint of betrayal in his tone.

"No—I mean—I was, but I'm renting my own place. And I got a job."

"Doing what?" he retorts.

Toby sighs, sitting on the single chair in his kitchen, leaning his elbow on the card table in front of him. "I'm waiting tables at a place near my house. It's paying really well so far—"

"Waiting tables? When you're a year out from finishing an engineering degree? Toby, you can't be serious—"

“Dad, I’ve got to go, I’m sorry. I should’ve told you sooner, but I wasn’t looking forward to...all of this.”

“All of what, Tob? Facing reality?”

“Yeah, ‘kay, Dad, I’ll talk to you later. I need to get ready for work,” he sighs, leaning back in the chair and stretching his legs.

“I really...I don’t know what else to say, Toby. We’ve given you every opportunity to succeed and it seems like you’re just throwing it all away.”

Holding his breath, Toby lowers the phone from his ear. “Love you, Dad,” he says hurriedly, hitting the red circle before he can change his mind.

CHAPTER 14

Opening the door, Jo is again disappointed by the face on her front step. "What do you want?" she snaps briskly, peeking through the shadows of her entryway into the misty morning air. This woman obviously doesn't take much pride in her appearance, she thinks, noticing an embarrassingly wrinkled shirt.

"Hey, Jo," the woman answers. "Do you recall telling Brett that he couldn't come in the house?"

Jo searches her memory, flushing slightly. It does sound vaguely familiar.

"That's why I'm here. Again," the woman sighs. "Brett was supposed to check in on you and give you a financial update, but I'm going to take care of that today, okay?"

Jo swings the door open wide. "I think I need some information from you," she says in a rush. "I need to see what's in my trust account."

The woman starts at Jo's sudden excitement for her visit. "Yep, that's the plan," she responds tentatively. "Can I come inside?"

Jo ushers her into her small entry and glimpses Precious already disappearing around the corner to the bedroom.

"I've printed off the monthly statement so you can see what money has been used," the woman says, making herself right at home on the sofa. Jo bristles at her immediate take-charge attitude. This is my home, and my account, she thinks. How did I lose all control in my life? I should have access to my own money, for goodness sakes.

"Jo?"

Her head snaps toward the woman's voice.

"Are you listening?" she asks, her short hair brushing her jaw as she turns toward her. She holds up a piece of paper in the space between them.

Moving around the coffee table, she sits next to the woman and nods.

"So, as I was saying," the girl continues, "this is what has come out this past month, and here," she points to the last page, "is the running balance."

Jo's eyes widen when she sees the bolded number at the bottom of the page. "That's all that's left?" she asks. "I don't see how that's possible. My late husband left me enough to live comfortably for years. This isn't nearly—" she sucks in a breath, the sound of blood rushing in her ears.

"Calm down," the woman says kindly, but Jo can barely hear her. "This isn't meant to be an argument, I'm simply showing you the most recent numbers from your bank account," she says, her hand brushing Jo's knee.

Jo recoils at her touch, her hands begin to shake. "I want you to leave," she commands, her voice low and almost unrecognizable in her own ears. Her chest feels as though it may burst.

"Jo, let me explain this in more detail, this isn't all—"

"Leave!" Jo shouts, ripping the paper from the woman's hands as tears begin to well in her eyes.

Frightened, the girl stands and abruptly moves away from her, searching for her shoes. Jo watches her struggle to slip them on her feet.

"I'm sorry," she thinks, but no words leave her lips. She sits there trembling, her nose beginning to run.

"This is why you are lonely, Jo," the woman shouts, clearly hurt. "You can't listen for two seconds to actually understand the situation! I'm done with all of this!" she cries, stepping out onto the step and slamming the door behind her.

Jo, with her head throbbing, flicks open the blind and watches the woman slump to the step and catch her face with her hands as her shoulders shake. Letting the blind fall back into place, Jo turns and faces the wall across from her. She stares, her arms motionless and limp, resting on the cushion. Taking a deep breath, she holds it as she watches the grey cattail tick rhythmically back and forth. Eventually, she lets it leave in a rush. Feeling her heartbeat return to normal, the tears start afresh. Shame fills her being as she imagines the woman's face as she left.

But those numbers...they couldn't be right. Walter had left her enough to live off of, hadn't he? Had she been using too much of it? Only paying for rent, a small cable bill, electricity, and a few meager groceries each week, she didn't see how that could be possible, given the number she had initially seen at the attorney's office years ago.

Laying across the couch, she pulls the quilt up to her chin. Precious' grumpy face appears from around the corner, purring in anticipation when she sees Jo in her typical spot. Taking her time, she saunters to the couch and eventually jumps on top of the quilt, settling in and patiently waiting for Jo to pet her.

. . .

"HEY, JO? YOU IN THERE?" Toby calls when his knock isn't answered immediately. "I can come back another time, but I don't have to work until the dinner shift. Thought we could watch *Days* if you're up for it."

Tapping his foot on the step, he waits for a few more minutes, then turns to leave. Just as he reaches the sidewalk, the door cracks open behind him.

"Hey," he says cheerily, spinning to find Jo peering out from behind her wooden barricade. His grin disappears when he registers the look on her face. Even in shadow, he can tell that something is deeply wrong. "Jo?" he asks, quickly retracing his steps toward the house. "Are you okay?"

She doesn't speak, but her eyes shift wildly from side to side, like a caged animal, looking for an escape. Her chest lifts and falls spastically.

"Hey, Jo, it's me. Toby," he grins, giving a small wave. "I know you probably don't recognize me with my beard. I promise I'm going to trim it back—or shave it off? Who knows. Probably tomorrow," he stalls, still not seeing an inch of recognition in her eyes. "I got distracted with this puzzle I pulled out last night and didn't have time," he continues, his feet fidgeting with the edge of the concrete step.

At the word 'puzzle', Jo's eyes finally connect with his and her pupils seem to shrink to a more appropriate size.

"Hey," he repeats again softly, tucking his curls behind his right ear. "You okay?"

"Toby?" she says, shuffling her feet on the welcome mat.

"Yep, that's me. Want to watch? Ooh, have you eaten yet? I brought some muffins," he comments, gesturing to the bag dangling from his outstretched hand. Jo nods, and moves out of the way for him to enter. Though her eyes are still troubled and her movements more stiff than usual, her demeanor begins to soften slightly once the door is closed.

"G'day Precious," Toby says as the fluffy cat winds around

his ankles, nearly tripping him as he makes his way past the coffee table. Jo follows him and sits awkwardly, as if her body has suddenly lost all flexibility. Toby flicks on the TV and passes her a muffin. Within minutes, her body seems to have mostly relaxed into the cushions, though she still hasn't said a word.

AFTER THE EPISODE, Toby is still distinctly aware of the change in Jo's energy. She didn't mutter judgements under her breath at all during the show—even during commercial breaks—nor did she get annoyed with Precious constantly changing positions on her lap. As he stands to pack up the extra muffins, he purses his lips, considering how he could possibly bring it up.

"I got angry with one of the workers today," Jo whispers.

Toby pauses and leans back, letting go of the muffin bag. "You did?" he asks in surprise.

"She came to show me my financials, but it was just like the other one—the number is far too low. Well," she caveats, "at least it seems like it couldn't possibly be that low considering how little I spend. I just don't see—"

"Did you get your account number? I could help you look at it so you could determine if something is amiss," Toby offers, recognizing the confusion on her face and desperately wanting to help. Jo simply shakes her head and looks down at her hands.

"Okay, well there's got to be some way for us to get it. What if I call down to the office or something? Or I could take you down there? I don't have a car anymore, but I'm sure I could figure out the bus schedule—"

"I don't trust them there. I think someone's been stealing from me, but if I say that, I know they're going to tell me I'm —" she stops short, sucking in a breath.

"You're what?" Toby asks gently.

Jo's eyes snap to his and he retreats involuntarily, slightly shocked at the intensity of her scowl.

"You know what, it's not important," he placates.

"It all started with that one man," she mutters under her breath, making Toby instantly feel more at ease. Her lack of audible internal dialogue was beginning to make him jittery.

"Which one?" he asks.

"I can't remember his name, but the one who used to do the reports with me."

"Oh, Brett?" Toby asks, amused. "The one you said you chased off?"

Jo nods. "Brett, right. That's him."

Toby considers for a moment, then resumes his position on the couch. "How do you think he did it?" he asks.

Jo appraises him, intrigued by the question.

"I mean, he really is in a perfect position to pull off something like that," Toby clarifies. "He has access to your records, he works with you regularly—so he's probably learned personal details about your life—and, he knows that you don't check your records in his absence," Toby lists, ticking off fingers as he goes. "Maybe he's been doing this for years."

"You—" Jo starts, then shifts uncomfortably, "you don't think I'm just being paranoid?"

"It doesn't matter what I think, Jo," Toby grins. "I'm your friend, and that means I'm here to help you."

"Alright," Jo nods, her shoulders lowering and her head lifting slightly.

"So what do you want to do about this?" Toby asks, leaning his head back on the edge of the sofa, his curls splaying out and framing his face.

Jo hesitates, considering this. She had never been asked to make a plan before. Well, at least not in the last twenty years. Everyone else makes the plans for her, based on what's practical at the moment—what 'will be best', as they usually explain. Is it possible that I've lost the ability to make plans? I don't have the faintest idea of where to start, she thinks. And then she thinks some more. Her thinking takes more time than she anticipated, and she begins to worry that she's boring Toby, but when she glances over, his eyes are closed. Had she been thinking so long that he fell asleep? How does one wake up a neighbor who has fallen asleep on your couch?

Toby suddenly opens his eyes and sits up, startling her, but she succeeds in masking her distress before he glances over.

"I wish I could get a personal investigator," she blurts out before he can say anything.

"Huh," he answers, scratching his chin. "You mean a private investigator? Those guys are pretty expensive, I think," he says to himself. Jo watches as he hunches forward and considers, resting his weight on his forearms. The beard really does make him look older.

He abruptly turns toward her, a mischievous look on his face. "Jo," he says, pausing for drama. "What if *we* did the investigating?"

Jo blinks. "I don't have any experience with that—" she begins.

"Neither do I!" he exclaims, "but it can't be that hard, right? I can Google it."

The blank stare on Jo's face causes Toby to burst out laughing, throwing his head back. "It means to look it up on the internet," he says between guffaws. Forcing himself to settle down, he continues, "It's okay, it's probably a crazy idea. We don't have to—"

"No," Jo cuts him off. "I want to try."

Toby stands up. "Then it's settled. My shift is early tomorrow, but I'll do some research tonight." Pausing, he looks at

Jo contemplatively. "Actually, better yet: why don't *you* do the research."

Again, Jo looks at him blankly. This time, with a slight sense of panic.

"C'mon, get up. Let's go," Toby says, motioning for her to stand. "We're going to the library."

CHAPTER 15

Jo hadn't realized that only three blocks in the opposite direction of the grocery store, there was a public library. Truly, she hadn't stepped foot in a building like this in over a decade. Ever since her eyes started to fail her, she had no use for reading.

Today, walking through the front doors fills her with anxiety as she scans the foyer, completely unsure where to go next. There doesn't seem to be a general check-in desk, just books and computers everywhere. Thankfully, Toby reaches for her hand and leads her to the elevator where they ascend a floor, then step out into a new section with a desk directly in front of the entrance.

"Hey," Toby greets the librarian. "Can you direct us to your section on private investigation?"

The woman gives him an odd look, but then begins typing something into the computer. Pulling out a slip of paper and a pencil, she writes down a series of numbers and letters, then hands it to Toby.

"There isn't a lot there, but hopefully should be what you're looking for," she says, pushing her glasses up.

"Thanks," Toby answers, briefly glancing at the numbers and then pocketing the paper.

"Follow me," he instructs Jo, then heads down the central aisle. Jo follows, but loses Toby midway through the stacks, not sure which aisle he turned down. Panic rises in her chest and she stops, turning in a small circle. If she can't find him, what should she do? Just keep looking around and hope to find the right spot? Go back to the librarian? That would be too embarrassing, she thinks. I could just sit on one of those chairs until I figure it out—

"Jo?" Toby calls, and she turns quickly toward his voice. He waves, a few aisles further down, and she walks purposefully toward him.

"Check this out," he says as she finally approaches. He points at a row of books and Jo adjusts her glasses, trying to read the small print.

"Let's grab a couple and you can read up on this while I work. Then we can decide what to do."

Jo nods. "I don't have a library card, though," she admits.

"That's okay," Toby waves her off. "I do. Just don't lose the books, because I don't have extra money for fines."

Jo blinks at him.

"I'm kidding!" Toby laughs. "I know you won't lose them." He reaches out and selects a few books, one with bright red lettering, one that seems to have seen better days, and one with a picture of what looks like a car salesman on the front.

"Alright," he says. "Let's go. I just need to pick up a hold before we check out."

Jo watches him navigate the different sections of the library, finding a book with his name printed on a slip protruding from the pages. She then follows him to a monitor with a scanner attached and observes with interest as he scans his card and then each book in turn. The last time she checked out a book at the library, there weren't any computers involved. She glances around, looking for any sign of rotating date stamps and card stock. Eventually, she follows Toby back out to the sidewalk and walks alongside him until they reach the house.

"What book did you check out?" Jo asks curiously, scanning the small stack in his arms.

"The one that I had on hold?" he asks.

Jo nods.

"Here, take a look," he says, slipping it out from between the other books and handing it to her. She stops walking and inspects the cover.

"Zen and the Art of Motorcycle Maintenance," she reads. "What is it?"

"Just a book about a father and son trip. A professor recommended it, but it took me a few months to remember to check it out. Kind of philosophical," he explains.

Handing it back to him, she returns to scanning the path in front of her for any obstacles as she steps forward.

"Do you ever read for fun?" he asks.

"It's been years," she admits. "After Walter…well, he would always get on my case about doing things that kept my mind active instead of wasting away in front of the television."

"How long has he been gone?" Toby questions gently.

"Twenty-two years."

Toby lets out a low whistle. "So you've been alone that long? Do you have any good friends around?"

Jo shakes her head. "I moved here ten years ago to be close to my daughter and left all of my lifelong friends," she explains, her shoulders slumping slightly. "That's not true," she corrects.

"That you came out to be close to your daughter?"

"No," she sighs. "That I left all my friends. I...haven't really been good at making friends for some time, and the ones I did have are either dead or wouldn't recognize me. I was alone back home in Minnesota, too."

"You're from Minnesota? That's where I'm from," Toby grins.

"You are?" Jo looks up in surprise.

"Yeah, I think I mentioned it when we first met, but I wouldn't expect you to remember that, especially because I barged in on you that first day."

Jo looks at him blankly, pausing mid-stride.

"When did you get connected with Simply Living?" Toby asks.

She furrows her brow, suddenly unsure. "It was...shortly after she died, I think?" Toby nods, gently placing a hand on her shoulder and leading her across the street.

"I'm sorry you've been lonely, Jo. And I'm sorry that in a neighborhood full of potential friends, people have been less than welcoming."

Blinking her eyes, she looks ahead and sees her house. Has it really been ten years? She pulls her cardigan around her chest and allows Toby to guide her to her walkway.

CHAPTER 16

"So?" Toby asks, standing on Jo's front step, still dressed in black slacks, a white collared shirt and a bow tie from his lunch shift. His black glasses seem to complete the ensemble, despite the fact that his long hair gives the unmistakable impression that he is a child playing dress up.

"So, what?" Jo asks, looking at him skeptically.

"What did you find in the books?" Toby asks expectantly. "Anything that will help us investigate?"

At this, Jo's eyes light up. "Yes!" she responds exuberantly, turning back into the house. Toby follows her through the open door and finds her rifling through the books on the coffee table. He notices the pens and note cards spread across the surface and grins to himself.

"There were a lot of good ideas," Jo mumbles, "but I think our best bet is to watch for a while first," she finishes, picking up the book she was looking for and turning to Toby. Her eyes are wide and attentive behind her tinted glasses.

"Sounds great," Toby says, impressed. "Watch like..."

"Like observe him in day to day life. Maybe then we can

find some sort of behavior that would tip us off to how he's stealing. Or how much he's stealing, if he's taking advantage of other people, too. Which, I bet he is," she adds. "They're never satisfied with just one take if they get away with it."

Toby nods. "Alright, when do you want to start?"

Jo's eyes shift nervously and her fingers twist around themselves.

"Is everything okay?" Toby asks gently.

She nods. "I...want to start today, but I wasn't able to find out where to start. Besides the fact that he works at Simply Living, I don't have any other information..." she admits, trailing off.

"I've gotcha covered," Toby says, pointing dramatically in her direction. "I called last night and found out when he's working today," he admits, glancing down at his smart watch. "He's got an evening shift, so he should be starting in about two hours. The only problem is figuring out a way to get down there. I kind of sold my car to rent this place and I haven't done much research on the bus routes—"

"I've gotcha covered," Jo mimics him, a mischievous grin on her face.

"I DIDN'T KNOW you had a car!" Toby exclaims as Jo attempts to pull the cover off of an old Buick in the back alley. He quickly steps in to help her, shaking off what looks like months—possibly even years—of dirt and dead leaves from the worn vinyl cover.

"I haven't had a license in years," Jo admits.

"Does it still work?" Toby questions.

"It did last time I used it."

Toby laughs, "Jo, you just informed me that you haven't had a license—"

"That doesn't mean I didn't drive it," she winks.

"Whoa, okay. I hadn't pegged you for a rule breaker," he says, grinning broadly. "Is it up to date on registration and insurance?" he asks, raising an eyebrow.

Jo shrugs.

"Well...let's hope we don't get pulled over then," Toby says, putting his hands on his hips. "Do you want to try starting her up?"

"You better do it," she says, handing him the keys and backing up a few steps.

"Hey, Jo! Toby!" a voice calls from the end of the alley, and both of their heads turn toward the interruption. Roy stands on the sidewalk, his freshly pressed khakis and light blue golf shirt looking pristine against the dirty fences. Jo's breath catches. When was the last time Roy said anything to her? Or even acknowledged her existence? Her right hand lifts and waves involuntarily. Taking this as an invitation, Roy walks up the alley toward her.

Jo turns frantically toward Toby, her eyes wide.

"You look nice, Jo," Toby assures her. "He's harmless."

"Roy is anything but harmless," she answers, her arms stiffly at her side.

"What is it with this guy," Toby comments, leaning on the driver's side of the car, glancing past Jo to observe Roy spryly walking along.

"Not helping," Jo mutters and Toby stifles a laugh.

"Is this your car?" Roy asks, close enough to speak at a normal volume. He admires the LeSabre, as if inspecting it for purchase.

Jo nods, adjusting the waistband of her pants.

"She's a beaut," Roy comments. "Where have you been, Jo? To be honest, I wondered if you'd moved out," he admits.

"I—"

"And why haven't you been back to Bunco?" Roy asks, turning an accusatory eye in Toby's direction.

Toby steps past Jo and claps Roy on the shoulder.

"I've got a job and Sunday's tend to be busy," he explains.

"They made an honest man out of you, eh?" Roy teases. "Where are you working? And, a better question is, do you always have to dress in a monkey suit?" Roy asks, lifting his pants along his surprisingly trim waistline and adjusting his walking cap.

"Oh this?" Toby asks, looking down. "I do actually have to wear this for work, but it's not that bad. I wait tables at Bob's."

"Down the street?" Roy asks, his eyebrows shooting up. "I love that place. Surprised we haven't seen each other there already."

"I've only been there for a couple of weeks," Toby explains, and Roy nods.

"Well, Jo, it's great to see you out and about," Roy says. "If you ever want to go for a walk or something, you know where to find me." He winks in Jo's direction, gently pats the trunk of the Buick and then retreats to the street. Jo watches him, her mouth hanging slightly open.

When Roy has covered enough distance to be out of earshot, Toby turns to Jo and raises his eyebrows.

"What?" Jo asks, tugging at her sweater.

"Seriously, what is it with all of you women and that guy? I get that he's good-looking, but—"

"It's not just that, Toby. Do you know who Roy is?"

Toby shakes his head. "Have you ever heard of LeMarc?"

"The cigar company?"

"He started it."

Toby's eyes widen. "Seriously?"

Jo nods. "He's loaded."

"Money and looks," Toby comments. "Something to aspire to."

Jo rolls her eyes.

"Let's see if she'll fire up," Toby says, pulling the door open and slipping into the driver's seat.

JO BREATHES DEEPLY and backs up a few more steps, remembering the day Walter bought this car for her. She was shiny and new then—barely fifty-five with surprising energy and a newfound freedom born from the rigidity of her youth. The car was used, but in pristine condition.

Her old Volkswagon had finally kicked the bucket after a few missed oil changes and an unfortunate run-in with a telephone pole. Not her fault, for the record. She had been pulling into the driveway when a little girl from down the street came tearing around the corner, her older brother in hot pursuit with a water balloon in his hand. Completely taken off-guard, Jo had swerved and somehow accelerated into the pole next to their driveway. When she informed Walter of the incident and showed him the car, he had laughed and asked why she didn't just hit the brakes. "Easy for you to say! You didn't have a three-year-old's life in your hands!" she had responded. That night, the neighbors stopped by with a plate of cookies.

Jo sighs. All's well that ends well. As Toby fires up the engine, the familiar sound hums through her.

He looks out the window at her, his eyes wide with excitement. "Does this sound right?" he asks. "I've never owned a car like this before."

"It sounds right," she shouts over the loud rumble of the V8 engine.

"Looks like you have almost a full tank of gas," he says, removing the key from the ignition, satisfied with the experiment. As the engine dies and silence surrounds her, Jo turns to walk back into the house.

"Hey," Toby calls after her. "Do you want your keys?"

"No, just keep them. You're the one with a license, remember?"

"Okay, sounds good," he says. "I'll go change and then we can leave in about thirty minutes? Is that too soon?"

She laughs at his obvious excitement, waves him off, and walks through the back door.

CHAPTER 17

"Is this what the book said?" Toby asks, passing Jo the ancient pair of binoculars. They work surprisingly well, considering they were likely manufactured during the First World War.

"It said that when doing reconnaissance, you need to hide in plain sight."

"Is...that what we're doing?" Toby questions, inspecting the branches next to his face.

Jo rolls her eyes. "Do you see any other 'natural' place for us to be loitering?" she asks with a flourish of her arm.

She has a point. The Simply Living office, though on a corner lot, isn't necessarily conveniently located. Positioned at the top of a dead-end hill, you definitely have to be *trying* to arrive here. Toby had parked the Buick closer to the neighborhood a block or so away in an attempt to be subtle. His heart rate has barely leveled out after helping Jo up the incline—substantially steeper than their regular route home from Trader Joe's.

"So now we wait," he states.

Jo nods resolutely, her eyes never leaving the front walkway. Though cars are parked near the front, nobody has entered or exited since they took their place in the Rose of Sharon foliage.

"He should be arriving any minute now," Toby comments, glancing at his watch.

The receptionist he had spoken with the day before was kind enough to explain the ins and outs of shift procedure. "Oh yes," she had assured him in a nasal, high-pitched voice, "Every employee checks in here at the main office before going out on home-visits. How else would they get their uniform?" She had laughed at her own joke, and Toby—ever unwilling to make things awkward—had laughed with her.

Suddenly, the sound of a car engine rises from the road below. Jo grips Toby's arm and pulls him lower in the bush as a blue Honda Civic screeches around the cul-de-sac and parks. A door slams, and though they can't make him out at first, Jo's grip tightens as they get a clear view of his profile from the walkway.

"Was that him?" Toby whispers after the man disappears into the building.

Jo nods. "That's him, alright." She adjusts her weight awkwardly and Toby reaches out a hand.

"Are you comfortable?"

"It's just part of being old. My knees are aching, that's all."

"Can you make it down the hill or should I go get the car and come back for you?"

"That would be a little obvious don't you think?"

Toby shrugs and follows Jo as she begins to amble along toward the sidewalk.

"Who knows how long he'll be in there," Toby comments. "We need to hurry."

"You're saying that as if I have any control over my speed at this moment," Jo says sardonically.

Eventually, Toby opens the passenger door and assists Jo

into the seat. Though she is clearly uncomfortable bending to slide through the door, once seated, she has plenty of room to find a comfortable position.

Quickly moving to the driver's side, Toby settles in behind the wheel and starts the engine. Literal moments later, the blue Civic appears in the rearview mirror.

"Now what?" Toby asks hurriedly.

"The book said to follow at least a few car lengths back," Jo instructs.

"And if there are no other cars on the road…"

"Then pretend there are," Jo blurts out, regretting that the book hadn't been more thorough.

Toby cautiously moves into the lane, being careful to keep his distance.

"I didn't take Tanner as a Civic guy," Jo comments under her breath.

Toby gives her a sidelong glance. "Huh?" he asks.

"I just didn't think he would drive something that flashy is all," she answers, adjusting her hair in the window reflection.

"Did you say 'Tanner'?"

Jo turns her head, her right hand still holding onto a white tendril gone askew. "That's the guy in the Civic," she says, an odd expression on her face.

"I thought his name was Brett," Toby explains, careful to turn left quickly enough to make sure they don't lose the car.

"Oh, right," Jo waves him off. "I'm not sure why that name was stuck in my head," she laughs, turning back to the window.

"It's for sure the right guy, though, right?" Toby asks, grinning nervously at the idea of them following the wrong Simply Living worker around town.

"It's him, for sure," she confirms.

Toby nods and relaxes slightly when another car pulls in front of him as they approach a stoplight. At least now it won't be glaringly obvious that they're in pursuit. Noticing motion in his peripheral vision, Toby looks over to find Jo pulling out a notebook from her shoulder bag.

"What's that for?" he asks.

"This," she answers excitedly, "is where I'm going to keep our notes for today. If we can follow him to all of his house calls and write down the addresses, then we could come back later and ask these people if anything has gone missing recently."

"Great idea," Toby says, only slightly alarmed at the idea of asking questions of complete strangers. When the Civic comes to a stop a few blocks later, Toby keeps their speed even and passes it, parking further down the street.

"Got it," Jo announces proudly, writing down the first house number. After making a few other marks on the paper, she closes the book and settles her hands over it in her lap. She inhales deeply and sighs contentedly.

"I haven't felt this alive in...well, years probably," Jo comments.

Toby grins, watching a girlish expression flicker across her face. Adjusting his glasses, he jumps as his phone buzzes in his pocket. Shoving his hand into his jeans to retrieve it, he almost hits his head on the ceiling of the car as his body stretches upward. Glancing at the screen, he hesitates.

"Aren't you going to answer it?" Jo asks, leaning back against the headrest. "He's going to be in there awhile, and I don't mind."

Toby considers this a moment as he stares at the screen, but then replaces the phone in his pocket. Not wanting to meet Jo's eyes, he clears his throat and busies himself by checking each and every window wiper setting.

"Who was that?" Jo asks quietly.

"Ummm, just my Dad," he answers guardedly, settling back into his seat and glancing into the rearview mirror to check on the Civic.

"Huh," Jo responds. "Not on good terms at the moment?"

"You could say that."

"Don't want to talk about it?"

Toby sighs. "It's not that I don't want to talk about it, it's just...it's complicated."

"My relationship with my Dad was complicated, too," she admits.

"Really?" Toby asks, turning toward her.

She nods, looking out the windshield at the trees lining the street. "The worst part is, I didn't ever get the time to figure out how to make it not complicated. He died when I was twenty-three."

"Oh wow, Jo, I'm so sorry to hear that."

She waves the comment off, pursing her lips. "No, it was a long time ago. I've come to terms with it. My Dad didn't approve of Walter, nor did he particularly agree with my getting married so young. Nevermind the fact that he and Mom got married at the exact same age," she chuckles.

"Why didn't he approve?"

"I grew up in a small town and Walter...his family didn't really fit in. They were transplants to the area and my Dad just really hadn't had much of a chance to get to know them." Jo pauses, pondering for a moment. "I think likely much of his apprehension was due to the fact that Walter planned to leave town and take me with him."

"He wanted you to stay?"

"He just didn't want anyone to do anything that made him nervous, especially not his daughter. I was thrilled. I'd been stuck in that town for long enough. And we were only going to Rochester, for goodness sakes."

"So you actually grew up in Minnesota?"

Jo nods. "Just outside of the Twin Cities, up until Walter and I got hitched. My Dad didn't really talk to us much after that. We would come home for holidays—spend a few days with both our families—and Dad was cordial. Mom thought that he would come around, especially when grand babies came along, but we didn't get the chance to try out that hypothesis. Cheri was born four months after he died."

Toby lets out a low whistle. "That's pretty tragic."

"It kind of is, isn't it?" Jo turns her head and looks at Toby. "My Dad and I didn't see eye to eye on plenty of things, but...I bet I could have found something if I'd been looking."

Toby nods, tucking his curls behind his ears. "It seems like nothing I do will ever be good enough for my dad," he admits. "I don't know how to find common ground when every single conversation comes back to how I'm 'wasting my life' or 'unwilling to put in the work'."

"And that's on him," Jo states resolutely, sitting up. "But you can't control what he does or says. He's just scared." She sighs, leaning back into the seat and closing her eyes. "Being a parent isn't intuitive, I'll tell you that. We come at life from a totally different perspective than our kids and somehow we have to find a way to relate. It's a wonder anyone gets along, really."

Toby laughs knowingly, then becomes more sober. "I lost my mom a few years ago. She was literally my best friend. So every time I talk to my dad…"

"It's doubly disappointing."

Toby nods.

"That's okay," she insists. "It's okay to be disappointed now. But you are both going to be different people in a year —maybe even in a week, as young as you are," she teases. "Sometimes patience and long-suffering is all we need," she concludes, patting his hand.

Suddenly, the blue Civic passes the driver's window in a blur and Toby jumps into action, starting the car and hastily pulling out after it.

"Here we go!" Jo exclaims excitedly, frantically gripping the dash.

CHAPTER 18

"Hey, Tob!" Clara calls from the kitchen as Toby runs through the door, pulling his hood off his head. Only slightly damp, he thinks, giving it a once over. He wasn't expecting rain when he left the house.

"Whose car is that?" she asks hesitantly.

"It's Jo's," he answers, jumping up the stairs two at a time. Glancing around for Ian and not finding him, his heart leaps slightly.

"She's letting you drive her car now?" Clara exclaims. "Toby, you remember what happened the other day, right?"

Toby nods, "Clara, Jo blew up because she doesn't trust anyone at Simply Living. If you're wearing that logo on your chest, you're immediately at a disadvantage."

"I get it, but I tried to explain everything to her kindly, and she wouldn't listen for two seconds. I honestly don't understand what she's getting so worked up about."

"She thinks that her balances are off," Toby explains. "She has this running ledger of expenses and the income she receives from her trust. I haven't looked at it closely, but she's sure that the numbers are fluctuating depending on the week."

"Well of course they are! The amount she gets is based on her expenses—which also fluctuate by the week. But she won't even hear me out."

"Do you think you could explain it to her before showing her the actual numbers? Maybe that's what's setting her off?"

"Maybe," Clara muses. "I also don't understand how she thinks we'd be able to take anything from that account. It's locked down. She gets her monthly stipend and, according to her will, any remainder goes to a cat shelter here in Portland when she dies. If someone was going to try stealing money from the elderly, she wouldn't be the easiest target."

"Doesn't mean it's impossible," Toby says.

"What if she suddenly gets it in her head that you're doing something dishonest, Toby? What if she calls the car in stolen because she forgot she lent it to you?"

"She wouldn't do that."

"Oh, so now you're the expert? I've been working with the elderly for over four years now, and suddenly you know more than I do?" she accuses.

"I'm not saying that you don't know what you're talking about...just that I know Jo."

"But you don't, Tob. You haven't been here for the worst moments, or seen all of the reasons why she doesn't have access to her own stuff. When I realized you had moved in next to her, I didn't ever think—"

"It's a good thing!" Toby insists. "She's getting out—we went to the library last night—and she's legitimately happier when I'm there. Did you know she doesn't have any real friends here? The people in her neighborhood are nice enough, they just aren't really *her people,* you know? That would make anyone grumpy."

Clara sighs. "I will admit, everyone at Simply Living is grateful for your involvement. We haven't had any angry calls in weeks."

"See? Helping."

Rolling her eyes, she fills up water glasses. "I still don't think it's the wisest choice for her to let you take her car."

"Hey, I'm a good driver!" Toby argues. "And it's not like I'm bumming off of her. She offered it to me when she heard I was planning to take the bus."

"You just casually mentioned that, I'm sure," Clara teases. Even her digging won't kill Toby's mood tonight, though. It was too much fun driving around town and playing spy. Though that's something he won't be divulging to Clara anytime soon. After his conversations with Jo in the car, he is rather more motivated than usual to put forth some effort in his family relationships, and that piece of info would likely kill the evening.

"How was work yesterday?" Toby asks, picking up bowls from the cupboard and setting the table.

"Good, good," Clara answers, distracted as she methodically measures out spices.

"No Ian tonight, then?"

"Nope, he had another commitment. Sorry about that. He told me about it the other day, and I completely forgot that Sunday night was out when we set this up."

I'm not sorry, Toby thinks. He still can't quite put his finger on what it is about the guy that makes him uncomfortable. Thinking about it now...perhaps it's the fact that he rarely smiles. Clara deserves someone who smiles.

"Talked with Dad today," Clara comments.

"How was that?" Toby asks, reaching into the silverware drawer.

"He said he's tried to call you a few times with no luck,"

she says meaningfully, turning to face him as she removes her apron.

Toby raises his eyebrows as he passes.

"Are you really just going to keep avoiding him?" she asks.

"I mean, I've already heard what he has to say," Toby answers, slumping down in his regular chair at the table.

"I think he's really worried about you," she explains, handing Toby a hot pad and moving back to the stove to retrieve the soup.

"I know," Toby sighs. "But it's not like I have any new information for him. Anything I say is just going to set him off again."

Clara nods, setting the pot on the table and sitting down. "Well, I have relayed the message," she says, pretending to wash her hands in mid-air. "The rest is up to you."

Toby nods. "Hey, has that employee appreciation thing happened yet?" he asks, Clara's miming reminding him that he needs to wash his hands before dinner.

"Still a few weeks away. Oh, that reminds me. I have a pass for the employee store if you need anything."

"What do they sell there?" he asks.

"Pretty much anything Nike you've ever wanted. Deeply discounted," she adds, raising an eyebrow.

"Hmmmm, tempting. Though I don't really need athletic wear."

"You aren't thinking of taking up running? You are in Portland now, after all."

Toby laughs. "Yeah, no thanks."

"Well if you change your mind, the offer stands."

"Thanks, Clar. And thanks for dinner."

"No prob," she says, ladling soup into her bowl. "I figured you could use a break from Italian."

"We do serve soup at Bob's," Toby teases.

"Not Mom's chicken noodle," she argues.

"True," he laughs, filling his bowl.

As soon as the first bite hits his lips, Toby is instantly transported back to his childhood living room...

EIGHT-YEAR-OLD CLARA KNEELS next to him, both setting up their dinner stations on top of the coffee table. They carefully lay out their settings, sliding toys and magazines to the side.

"Not like that," Clara instructs, flipping over Toby's fabric placemat and arranging his cutlery on the proper sides. Mom is in the kitchen, and the comforting smell of chicken noodle soup wafts through the open door.

"I love it when Dad works late," Toby grins, taking a sip of his water and carefully placing the plastic cup back on the mat.

"I know. Eating in the living room is the best," Clara giggles.

"Are you two ready for soup?" Mom calls from the kitchen.

"Yes!" they both exclaim eagerly.

"Alright, it's a little hot," she cautions, moving into the room and setting their bowls in front of them. She immediately exits and retrieves her own bowl from the kitchen, then curls her legs under her and sits on the floor next to Toby. He blows on each bite—meticulously avoiding the celery—and notices how his mother always tucks her curls behind her ears before she takes a bite.

"TOB?" Clara asks, looking at him quizzically.

"Huh?"

"You're just staring at your spoon. Is there a hair in the soup or something?" she questions, winking at him and taking a bite.

"No, no," Toby laughs, placing the spoonful of soup in his mouth. "I was just...remembering."

CHAPTER 19

Jo had insisted that Toby take the car to visit his sister. That thing has been sitting out back collecting dust for years, she thinks. It's about time that it fulfills the measure of its creation. She hadn't expected it to start up as quickly as it did, to be honest. Perhaps those years of religious oil changes actually did make a difference? Live and learn.

Walking into the kitchen, she reaches down to pet Precious, who is already predictably weaving around her feet. Time for dinner. Pulling a can from the cupboard, Jo opens it and empties it into a bowl. As Precious begins lapping it up, Jo turns back in search of something that seems appetizing. More and more frequently, she isn't able to find anything that appeals to her. Especially for dinner.

Settling on a piece of toast, she pulls the bread from the fridge. Opening the bag, she gingerly pulls out a slice and pops it in the toaster, then turns to see that Precious has already left the kitchen. Her bowl isn't even empty yet, she notices, her eyebrows furrowing. Hopefully my pickiness isn't contagious, she thinks.

The toaster dings and Jo spins to retrieve her meal. Sighing at the lack of bread peeking from the top, she reaches for a fork. How is it possible that bread shrinks this much when toasted? The crust sits just below the edge of the toaster, leaving too much space for Jo's fingers to get burned whilst reaching in. She cautiously presses the fork tines to the edge of the piece, then pulls upward. Though it takes a few tries, she eventually flips the bread from its metal confines onto her plate.

"Gotcha," she announces proudly. Opening the fridge, she pulls out a jar of grape jelly. Carrying it back to her plate, she runs into something on the floor and gasps.

"What is that doing there?" she gripes, recognizing one of Precious' empty food bowls. Setting the jar on the counter, she reaches down and stops. This bowl has food remnants in it. Her eyes flit between this bowl and the dish Precious was just eating out of. I clearly remember picking up the breakfast bowl this morning, Jo thinks, thoroughly flummoxed. Shrugging, she picks up the dirty dish and sets it in the sink, then slowly makes her way into the living room to turn on her evening programs.

"Jo?" Toby calls through the door. Though they had planned to get together this morning, he hadn't thought to stop by and confirm the day before. With work being so busy, he hadn't even said as much as hello to Jo in three days.

Eventually, footsteps inside indicate that she's approaching the door. When it swings open, Toby smiles.

"Good morning," he greets her happily, and Jo's eyes light up. "You did remember we were going questioning today, right?" Toby teases, taking in her lack of pants.

"You shaved," she comments blandly.

"You're wearing makeup," he retorts, noticing a slight

shade of blue above her eyelids. Jo waves him off and retreats toward her bedroom. Shaking his head, Toby turns and sits on the concrete step, the cold from the surface immediately beginning to seep through his pants. He breathes deeply, taking in the sights of the morning. A fine mist rises from the blades of grass as the sun stretches across the yard. Birds dart between the branches of the large oak tree in the neighbor's yard, singing to each other as they pass. A perfect morning, Toby thinks, his body shedding some of the tension trapped there from the last three days.

"We'll be there Saturday," his father had said. Saturday. A pang of anxiety rushes through Toby's gut just remembering the lilt in his father's tone. This is always how it happens, he thinks. I get excited that Dad and Carole are making the effort to visit, but then it inevitably turns into some type of intervention. He sighs, running his hands through his curls. At least this time Clara will be here to divert some of their attention.

The door squeaks behind him, and he quickly jumps up. Jo's backside presses against the glass as she attempts to turn the key in the lock. Toby steps down to the sidewalk, shoving his hands in his pockets and waiting patiently for her to finish.

"Ready?" he asks as she grasps the handrail.

"Of course I'm ready," she says under her breath, cautiously moving her right foot to the next step. Toby watches nervously as her knees shudder under pressure each time she moves downward, forcing himself to remain put. When she reaches the bottom, he breathes a sigh of relief.

"So where to first?" he asks, opening the passenger door for her.

As she laboriously clambers through the door, she assures him, "I've got the list."

Toby nods, a smile playing at the corner of his mouth. Of course she does.

PULLING up in front of the first house, Toby can almost feel the uncertainty permeating Jo's demeanor. Putting the car in park on the wrong side of the road, he turns to her and finds wide eyes staring back at him. Despite his best efforts, he bursts into laughter. Jo, taken aback, stares at him as he attempts to reign it in.

"I'm sorry!" he splutters. "You just look terrified!"

Jo's face sours. "I am not!"

"Well your face says otherwise," he teases, lifting his glasses to wipe his eyes. "I'm sorry, I don't know why I laughed so hard. It was just—"

"Alright, alright," Jo cuts in seriously, straightening her button-up blouse. "I might be slightly nervous," she admits.

Toby nods, straightening his hair. "I mean, it *is* kind of weird. Knocking on random people's doors. We don't have to—"

"Yes we do!" Jo asserts. "If he's stealing from other people, too, it's my responsibility to get to the bottom of this."

Toby opens his door. "Well alright then! Let's do this!" he shouts triumphantly, pumping a fist in the air. Jo swings her door wide and with impressive confidence, steps to the street —her white hair bobbing with each movement—and nearly struts around the front of the car, notebook in hand.

Allowing her to take the lead, Toby meanders along the paving stones behind her, gratefully noting the lack of a stairway leading to the front door. Jo navigates the slight step up to the modest porch and, without hesitation, rings the bell.

After a moment, the door opens. An elderly man stands

behind the screen door staring at them. His large glasses, combined with his bushy eyebrows, make him seem owl-like as he peers from behind the glass.

"Whad'ya want?" he asks gruffly, shifting his weight to his good hip.

"Hi. I'm Jo, and I think we have the same care-giver through Simply Living?"

"Huh?" the man asks, tilting his good ear toward the door.

"Simply Living," Jo shouts. "I think Terrance—"

"Brett," Toby corrects.

"Brett—is stealing from me. You know, the caregiver?" she explains.

The man looks at her quizzically. "Things have gone missing?"

Jo nods. Toby admires the pearlescent snaps on the man's collared shirt.

"Well, come in then," he mutters, moving to open the screen. "And who're you?" he asks, as if noticing Toby for the first time.

"Toby, I'm Jo's neighbor," he answers quickly.

"Fine," he nods, shuffling back and allowing them to cross the threshold.

"What's your name?" Toby asks, once the door is shut behind him.

"Gary," he grunts, attempting to lift his pants back into place, only to have them slowly settle under his protruding belly once again. "Do you want to sit down?"

To Toby's surprise, Jo nods and follows him into the living room. The shades are drawn low over the windows, making the interior of the house seem almost cave-like. Though he can't be completely sure, it looks like the carpet is an odd shade of green. He attempts to keep his face blank as he surreptitiously takes in their surroundings.

"So Gary," Jo starts, settling into the well-worn couch cushion. "Have you had things go missing, too?"

"Sure have," he nods resolutely.

Jo's eyes light up with the excitement of having found a connection. "When did you start noticing?" she asks energetically.

"Well..." Gary starts, looking up at the ceiling and rubbing the scratchy stubble on his chin. "I probably started noticing it right after my wife left me. But I think it's been happening longer."

Jo's face puckers in confusion. "Your wife left you recently?" she asks.

"If you consider 1987 recently," Gary laughs.

"Was Simply Living caring for you then?" Jo asks, not amused.

"Are you kidding? I didn't need anyone to care for me then," he exclaims. "Truth be told, I don't need anyone caring for me now, either, but my grandkids insisted—"

"So you haven't had *more* things go missing since hiring Simply Living? Or since Brett has been your caregiver?" Jo asks, cutting him off.

Gary looks at her blankly. "What would that have to do with it? The aliens don't care who's in the house."

Toby coughs into his elbow to conceal a burst of laughter. Placing his other hand on Jo's shoulder, he doubles over, curls flying around his face.

"Is he going to be okay?" Gary asks in genuine concern.

"Oh, yes," Jo answers. "Must have gotten something caught in his throat."

"Yes," Toby chokes. "Sorry about that," he says, his voice still hoarse. He stands, his face red and eyes watering. "Jo, I think we should be on our way. Gary, thanks so much for letting us ask a couple of questions—"

"I can tell you more about the things they've taken from me," he offers, standing and adjusting his pants. Jo follows suit and stands across from him, still quizzically assessing the man. Toby immediately grips Jo's arm and leads her toward the door.

"Maybe some other time," Jo responds kindly. "I think Toby here needs to get going to—a—what was it you had again today?" she asks, scrambling.

"Work," Toby answers seriously. "Have to get going to work."

Letting go of Jo, he pushes the door open and steps out onto the landing. Jo follows, carefully navigating the threshold by bracing her arm against the doorframe.

Gary nods. "Well stop by anytime. I'm sorry they've gotten to you, too," he says apologetically.

Jo thanks him, then follows Toby down the walk. Once safely in the car, Jo's face nearly cracks as laughter erupts out of her, her entire body shaking. Toby can't help but laugh with her. With tears still streaming down her face, Jo removes her glasses and begins to wipe her cheeks. Incredibly, her blue eyeshadow still seems to be completely intact.

"He thought we wanted to know about aliens?" Jo manages to squeak out, barely holding in another fit of laughter.

"I know, I barely avoided laughing directly in his face when that came out of his mouth," Toby admits, attempting to stretch his stomach muscles in the cramped space. "That. Was. Amazing," he says, sighing and leaning his head back against the seat.

Jo, breathing deeply, pulls out her notebook. "But we're not any closer to finding out whether Brett has done this before," she says, disappointment in her tone.

Toby grins, lifting in his seat. "Hey, you remembered his

name!" he congratulates her, and she swats at him with her pen.

"It's true, though. We're back at square one," he continues. "On to the next one?"

Jo nods as he puts the car in gear.

CHAPTER 20

"Hey," Toby answers, his voice sounding abrasive in the silence of his kitchen.

"Sorry to call so late," Clara apologizes.

"No prob, I had to close tonight," he yawns.

"Isn't that three nights this week?"

Toby nods, walking into the living room and dropping into the beanbag chair. "Yep."

"Why are they having you work so many late shifts?"

"It's not their fault, I kind of requested it."

"Oh, for some reason I thought—"

"It's just because I've been helping Jo during the day. Normally I would prefer to work lunch at least a few times a week, but she's got this plan—"

"You mean her plan to bring down Simply Living?"

Toby laughs. "Not all of Simply Living."

"Just Brett?" Clara teases.

"Pretty much."

"And how have you been going about helping her with this plan?"

Toby hesitates. "Ummmm....I think it's best if I kept that to myself," he chuckles.

"Toby, you aren't doing anything illegal, right? If you get in trouble with the law, I think Dad is going to have a heart attack. Literally."

Still pressing the phone to his ear, Toby leans his head against the soft fabric of the bean bag chair and closes his eyes. "I promise, nothing illegal," he assures her.

"But you still won't tell me what this plan is? Toby, you know that Jo—"

"Clara, it's totally fine. She's super into it and she's doing all the research herself. It's not like I'm planting ideas in her head. I'm just driving her around and providing moral support."

Clara sighs. "I just don't understand why you can't encourage her to do normal 90-year-old hobbies. Like knitting. Have you asked her if she likes knitting?"

Toby grins. "I keep trying to get her to come to Bunco with me, but it's a no-go."

"Are you still doing that?"

"It doesn't work out often that I have a Sunday evening off, but I went again last week. It's hilarious, Clar. You'd get a kick out of it."

"I can't believe your best friends have an average age higher than our parents," she scoffs, but her voice radiates warmth. "Maybe sometime."

"I really think you should come on a ride with me and Jo, too."

"Toby, that would be a terrible idea. If she recognized me..." Clara trails off.

Laughing, he stretches out his legs and puts one arm under his head. "Yeah, you're probably right."

"Well you didn't need to agree *that* quickly," she mutters.

Even while bantering back and forth with Clara, Toby can

feel his eyelids growing heavy. Though his body protests, he pulls himself upright. "Clara, I'm fading fast. I assume you wanted to talk about Dad?"

"Yep, sorry, I'll be quick. He texted and asked about a few things. Are you okay joining us on an outing or two? Obviously if it works with your schedule. I just didn't know how you were feeling—"

"No, that's fine. I'll text you my shifts and if it works, I'll plan to be at whatever."

"You sure?"

Pausing, Toby questions whether he is sure or not. "Yes," he sighs. "I'm sure. Just promise me that if he starts to rant about anything relating to life goals, you'll find a worthy distraction."

"I promise I'll try," she agrees. "I'll shoot you over some tentative plans in the morning."

"Cool. And Clara?"

"Uh-huh?"

"I really do want to introduce you to Jo. I think she's in a good place. And without a logo on your chest, you might have a chance at making a good impression."

Clara doesn't respond immediately and for a moment, he wonders if his joke crossed the line.

"I'll consider it. Goodnight Tob."

"'Night," he answers, ending the call.

Stumbling to the bathroom, he hastily brushes his teeth. Jo wouldn't be opposed to meeting someone new if he introduced them, right? His mind returns to the first time he interacted with her outside her door. It wasn't that bad. As he flops into bed and pulls the covers over his shoulders, he muses on potential scenarios. It has to happen, he thinks. I just have to find the right opportunity...

CHAPTER 21

"This isn't really what I had in mind," Jo complains, staring stubbornly out the passenger side window.

"Hey," Toby argues, "you said you wanted to see Brett in real-life situations."

"I know, but I didn't think—what kind of person goes roller-skating on their day off?"

Toby stifles a laugh. "Jo, I promise, I looked for other options, but everything else would have been too suspicious. Us randomly showing up at his bank or country club?"

"He belongs to a country club?" Jo asks in shock, turning to Toby with wide eyes.

"I thought I told you that."

"You most certainly did not," Jo accuses. "He doesn't make nearly enough to afford something like that."

"Well, depending on the membership—"

"And why couldn't we show up there?" she continues.

"Because it's on the other side of town! Why would we ever have reason to go there? And everything else was just too inconsistent. Sure, he goes to the grocery store, but we would have to watch him for weeks to nail down a pattern on that. And according to my sources, he never really goes to the same bar on the weekends. Plus, he knows you don't stay up past six," Toby points out.

"But roller skating?" Jo whines.

"He does it every week. Apparently his girlfriend is a fan. Did you know she works at Simply Living, too?"

"Not surprised," Jo snorts. "They're probably both in on it."

Again, Toby forces his face to remain calm. "We don't have to do this, you know. Why do you want to see him outside of work anyway?"

Jo gives an exasperated huff. "Because I want to see how he responds when he sees me. And I want to see how he acts around other people *before* he sees me. I've been researching red flags."

"Red flags for what?" Toby asks grinning.

"For narcissists, manipulators, you know. The gamut."

Toby puts the car in park and removes the key from the ignition, turning toward her. "Where have you been finding this info?"

Jo turns to face him, a twinkle in her eyes. "The library."

Toby's jaw drops. "You've been to the library? On your own?"

"Once I was even there past six," she says conspiratorially. "Now stop lallygagging," she commands, gripping the handle of her door and pushing it open with her right foot.

"Game on," Toby says, opening his door and stepping out into the parking lot. "But I'm only putting on skates if you do."

"When I break a hip, it's your fault," Jo says under her breath.

. . .

As they enter the roller rink, Toby walks next to Jo up the slight carpeted incline toward the ticket booth. The building smells of sweat and old popcorn, but the neon lightning bolts in the black carpeting—on the floors and walls—make up for it.

As they approach the window, a heavy-set man with a black ponytail comes into view. Surprisingly, Jo keeps her comments to herself, though Toby can see her assessing everything from the man's eyebrow piercing to the scantily clad cartoon on his t-shirt.

"Two, and we need rentals," Toby quickly speaks, and the man glances at a dirty, torn price sheet near the register.

"Fourteen," he says, and Toby pulls out his credit card.

"You don't have to pay for me," Jo says.

"When's the last time you let a guy pay for you to go roller skating?" Toby asks as the man rips two tickets from an enormously large green spool of raffle tape.

Jo stares at him, and for a second, Toby wonders if he's said something wrong.

"Are you okay?" he asks worriedly.

She shakes her head. "The last time I went roller skating was with Walter when I was seventeen."

Toby lets out a low whistle. "Then I have a lot to live up to, I guess."

Jo retrieves the tickets through the hole in the glass and turns to Toby. "That time ended with my first kiss, so I don't think living up to it is possible," she says, raising an eyebrow.

"A guy can try, can't he?" Toby laughs.

The sound of techno music hits them as soon as they pass through the door into the area surrounding the rink. With low lighting and plenty of people abuzz around them, Toby begins to wonder whether they'll even be able to find Brett in the crowd. Who knew that roller skating was still a thing?

Moving to the counter, he asks for his size skate and encourages Jo to do the same.

"I haven't bought shoes in five years," she states. "I have no idea what size I am."

Kneeling down, he checks the bottom of her shoe and thankfully finds the number quite effortlessly. "Nice try," he teases. "I won't be thwarted that easily."

Jo rolls her eyes and cautiously walks to an oversized, carpeted round platform that everyone else seems to be using as a seat to lace up their skates.

The girl behind the counter—who looks to be about fourteen, despite her thick liquid eyeliner—lazily scans the shelves for their sizes, eventually settling on two tan pairs of skates. She sets them on the counter and pops her gum.

"Thanks," Toby says, picking them up and walking toward Jo.

"The pink laces really add something," Jo comments, assessing Toby's pair.

"They're really 'me'," he states and Jo laughs, despite her best efforts to remain surly about the whole situation.

"Want me to help you put these on?" he asks, nearly yelling over the thumping bass.

"You're going to have to. My spine doesn't bend that way anymore. Why do you think I only own slip-ons?"

Toby grins and begins to loosen the laces. "Left foot, please," he instructs and Jo obediently slips the shoe from her foot and points her toe into the boot of the skate.

Though it takes some finagling, eventually Toby sits back to admire his handiwork. Jo's polyester pants fall over the tops of the skates, obscuring the laces. At least the bright pink ones weren't wasted on her pair.

Toby picks up their shoes and takes them to the cubbies near the rental desk. He takes his time, giving Jo a moment to process. Suddenly, an idea occurs to him and he glides over to the counter.

When he returns, he finds Jo staring at her legs outstretched, in disbelief that there are actual skates securely attached to her feet.

"I'm going to die," she says, her glasses reflecting the neon lights overhead.

"You are not going to die, because I," he announces grandly, "got you this." With a flourish, he swings a small frame of PVC pipe on wheels around his legs and sets it in front of Jo.

"How can I ever thank you?" Jo asks, her voice flat.

"Do you even know what it is?"

Jo shakes her head.

"This is to help you skate. So you don't fall, and therefore don't break a hip," he announces proudly. "Think of it like your grocery cart."

"How is this going to keep me from falling? It has wheels, too," she notices skeptically.

"Just try it," he insists, helping her up and placing her hands on the bars. "Practice around the carpeted area first while I finish lacing up my skates. Then we can try the actual rink."

Toby suppresses a grin as Jo hesitantly begins moving her legs back and forth. For a brief moment, panic grips his chest at the thought of Jo falling violently and severely injuring herself. But how bad could it really be when she's leaning on that frame? Brushing it off, he focuses on tightening the neon laces around his ankles and then stands to join her. Surprisingly, Jo is nowhere to be found. He finally finds her clear across the room next to the wall of the rink. Toby watches her scan the skaters, her eyes darting between the moving figures.

On wobbly legs, he moves to the wall beside her. "Find

him yet?"

"Not yet. You're sure he's here?"

"Jo, you watched him drive into the parking lot."

She nods, still unconvinced, and continues to scan the crowd. Turning his head, Toby notices the smiling faces and outbursts of laughter between teens on the floor. Two girls skate along the boards, giggling and moving forward awkwardly as they grab each other's arms for support. His attention snaps to a man near the back of the rink, his hand pressed against the wall. A girl with long blond hair skates near him, practicing spins as he watches. Could that be Brett? In the low lighting, it's difficult to be sure, but it's a definite possibility.

Toby lifts his hand and points, catching Jo's gaze. She squints, lifting her glasses and replacing them.

"Is that him?"

"I'm not totally sure, but I think it could be."

"Are they just sitting back there?"

Toby nods. "Seems like she's practicing or something."

Jo heaves a sigh. "So we have to skate," she states matter-of-factly.

Toby laughs and places a hand on her shoulder. "We don't *have* to do anything, Jo. They'll have to come off the rink eventually."

"No, that will just prolong the annoyance of listening to this terrible music," she mutters—squeezing her eyes shut for added drama—and begins to move toward the gap in the boards.

Toby goes first, carefully allowing his weight to settle on each set of wheels as he touches them to the slick wooden floor. Gripping the boards tightly, he helps lift the skating aid over the lip, then places one foot in front of it to keep it from rolling away from the entrance. Jo reaches out, reminding Toby of a child first learning to walk. Putting all her weight on the PVC pipes, she waits. Staring at her skates, she takes two deep breaths and then cautiously lifts her left foot. One at a time, she places her skates on the rink surface. Her shoulders visibly relax as she realizes she is still standing upright. White-knuckling the frame, she shifts her feet forward and back, making slight forward progress.

"You're not wasting any time, are you?" Toby laughs, moving his foot to allow her to push the frame further. Turning, and with a hand still using the board edges as a guide, he skates next to her. "This isn't so bad, right?"

Jo doesn't answer, solely focused on not falling. Instead of continuing to distract her, Toby lifts his head and experiences the brightly colored chaos surrounding him, all while keeping a watchful eye out for anyone that may inadvertently run into Jo. One man in particular catches his eye. Dressed as if he just stepped out of a time machine from the 70's, he whirls around the rink—his skates weaving around each other in intricate patterns, making it look as if his ankles are made of rubber. His feathered hair waves in the self-made breeze and Toby can't take his eyes off of his hands, moving perfectly in time with the beat.

"There's always one," Jo says, loud enough to be audible over the music.

"Huh?" Toby asks, moving his head closer to her.

"There's always that one guy," she repeats. "The guy that loves roller-skating so much that he can't find a better use of his time."

"Being active seems like a good use of spare time," Toby counters.

Jo grunts. Having made it around the bend, they begin up the straight section and Toby's eyes widen when he sees that the boards are ending in a few feet, giving way to straight wall.

"Hey," he says, "you said you had your first kiss last time

you roller skated?" he shouts, attempting to distract himself as his hand passes his last, solid hand-hold.

"Well, it wasn't the last time I roller-skated," she clarifies. "Just the last time a guy paid for me."

"You and Walter never went skating again?

"We did, but we were married then. It didn't quite seem like he was paying for me since it was a joint decision to use the money."

"You had a say in how your money was spent?" Toby asks.

Jo stops, staring at him incredulously.

"Okay, okay," he laughs, adjusting his glasses with his free hand. "It just seems like a lot of couples back then...well, that the men kind of made all the decisions."

Jo waves him off. "It wasn't like that for everyone. People look at our relationships then and say that we women didn't know that we were being stifled. It was a simpler time, and I was happy."

"Do you think everyone was?"

"Do you think everyone is now?"

Toby nods in understanding. "So how often did you and Walter go roller-skating?"

"Maybe a couple times a year? During the 70's it was all the rage, but that was mostly for the wilder crowd. I had more important things to be worrying about at home."

Toby looks up to see the wall curving again, then glances across the width of the rink to find the couple they had spotted earlier. The woman, with arms outstretched toward the man, is attempting to teach a couples dance step. The man, his back to them, doesn't seem to be picking up on it very quickly.

"Should we just skate up next to them?" Toby asks. "If we follow the wall, that should at least give us a good view of his face as we turn."

Jo nods, picking up her pace ever so slightly. As they

approach, Jo lifts her head and stares at the man, as if willing him to look her direction. They move closer, and Toby strains to hear the conversation over the pulsing beat. Suddenly, one of his legs slips out from under him and he frantically waves his arms, attempting to gain his balance. His skates fly toward the ceiling and he plummets to the ground, landing hard on his backside, kicking Jo's skating aid as he falls. The frame whirs to the boards on the other side of the bend, leaving Jo frozen in fear.

The couple, having been distracted by the commotion, stares at the odd sight in front of them. A young man with curly hair and boxy glasses, flat on his back next to an elderly woman, slightly bent at the waist, with arms outstretched and eyes wide. Having watched the frame go flying, the man quickly retrieves it and places it under Jo's hands.

Toby sits up just as this exchange takes place and witnesses the recognition that follows.

"Are you okay?" the man asks, then suddenly freezes when he meets Jo's eyes. Jo watches him with intensity, not saying a thing. "Oh, hey, Jo, right?" he says, standing up and backing away slightly.

"You know her?" his girlfriend asks.

"Well, I've met with her a few times," he admits. "Through work."

"More than a few," Jo challenges. "You've been managing my finances for years," she says, hunched over the PVC pipes. Her white hair seems to change the colors of the rainbow with the flashing lights. With his tailbone still burning, Toby stares at the two of them.

"Well, I don't really manage anything, I just—"

"You have the password to my online banking don't you?" she says, her voice accusatory.

"Yes, but only—" the man stops, looking between Jo and Toby. "Wait, are you even allowed to be here?"

"Why wouldn't I be?" Jo asks.

"It's kind of a dangerous activity," he says, then looks at Toby. "Did you bring her?"

Toby nods, shifting slightly toward the edge of the rink so he can use the wall to lift himself to his feet.

"You realize that this isn't safe for someone who—" he starts, skating toward Toby, but Jo cuts him off.

"For someone who? What, Brett? Are you going to make up more stories about how I'm not lucid? How I shouldn't be left alone to care for myself? I'm obviously doing just fine," she retorts, straightening her t-shirt over her stretchy waistband.

Toby gropes the wall, carefully placing his weight over one knee as he stands. "Hey, Jo, let's let them get back to their...well, whatever you were doing before we interrupted."

Jo nods resolutely and lifts her nose into the air as she begins to skate forward again. She's getting faster, Toby thinks, as he makes his way past the final few feet of wall to grasp the boards again. He smiles nervously at Brett as he passes, then glides to catch up with Jo.

"So?" he asks when he is within earshot.

"So, what?" she replies, her eyes trained on the exit door.

"Was that what you were hoping for?"

"It told me everything I needed to know."

Toby grins at the stubborn glint in her eyes. "Well I'm glad we came, then."

The DJ's voice booms over the rink, "Aaaaaalright, it's time for limbo!!! Come out and join us on the floor to see how low you can go!"

A cheer rises from the crowd and Toby looks to Jo. "Want to play?"

"Just get me out of this death trap, will you?" she hisses, looking disgusted at the flow of people entering the rink.

"Got it," Toby says, suppressing a laugh.

CHAPTER 22

"I sit people table ten for you," the hostess says in broken English, passing by Toby at the computer monitor.

"Perfect, thanks," he says without allowing his eyes to stray from the screen. His section is almost full and it's only 5:15. Not the typical Thursday.

"Pretty busy tonight," a voice says behind him. Not recognizing it, he turns. A girl with freckles and black curly hair stands next to the bar, waiting patiently for her drink order to be filled.

"Are you a new hire?" he asks. "I know Dave mentioned we had some new servers coming on, but I haven't overlapped shifts with anyone yet."

"Yep, just finished training on Monday."

"Cool, he says," turning back to the computer and entering in his last appetizer. She's cute. Maybe twenty, he thinks.

Finishing his order, he turns. "Yes, definitely busy tonight," he answers her original question. "Do you need help with anything?"

"No, I think I got it. I've worked at other restaurants, so it's kind of all the same."

Toby nods. "I'm Toby," he says, reaching out a hand.

She shakes it and her nose wrinkles a little when she smiles. "Abby."

"Welcome to the team, Abby," he grins. Pulling his hand away, he adjusts his apron. "I'm sure I'll see you around."

She nods and turns back to the bar. For a moment, he searches his brain for his next task. Table ten, right, he thinks, walking toward the dining room.

"You did what!?" Clara exclaims, setting her glass of water on the table and flouncing down in her chair dramatically. "Toby, that could have been really dangerous."

"I think she had fun, actually. She wouldn't admit it, but she seemed...lighter somehow when I dropped her off."

Clara taps her fingers on the glass, pursing her lips. "Don't you think this has gone a bit far?"

"How so?" Toby asks, crossing his legs and leaning back in the chair.

"Tob, seriously?"

He looks at her, not sure how to respond.

"This is all just...pure crazy! Jo isn't all there, Toby. She lashes out at anyone and everyone, she makes up stories that are clearly not factually based, and now you're egging her on! If Brett found out that you were purposefully stalking him—"

"It's not stalking...more like observing—"

"It's full on stalking, Toby," Clara asserts, standing and beginning to pace. "And I get that Jo is doing well—I mean, honestly, better than well, considering—but it seems like entertaining her ideas is only going to cause her more harm in the long-run."

Toby runs his hands through his hair. "Regardless of

whether what she believes is true, it clearly hasn't been helping her for people to tell her that. *So what* if her ideas are a bit quirky? Or if her plans don't make complete sense? Would it be more beneficial for me to *tell* her she has to get out and be active and have her resent me for it? That's what all the workers do! What harm can really come from me doing what she wants?"

"Toby, you had an elderly woman on roller skates yesterday. She could have killed herself. Someone could have sued you, and—"

"Nobody is going to sue me," he scoffs. "She has nobody, Clara. Literally nobody. It's me, her cat, and her television. But this week, she was outside for hours, she did something she hasn't done since the 70's and she has all kinds of confidence from feeling like she has control over her life!" he asserts, and the intensity of his voice is shocking to both of them. He clears his throat. Clara stands in the middle of the kitchen, hands on her hips, pondering.

"Come meet her with me," Toby says gently. "I think seeing us together will make you feel more comfortable with me spending so much time with her. You'll see that it's harmless."

Clara meets his eyes just as the doorbell rings. Toby inhales slowly as Clara walks around the half-wall and down the few stairs to the entryway.

"Hey, babe," Ian says as she opens the door. "Sorry I'm late, got held up."

"No, it's fine," she says, resting her head on his shoulder as he embraces her.

"Everything alright?" he asks, leaning back to look at her face.

"Yes, sorry, just a long day," she says, retreating back up the stairs.

"Hey Toby," Ian waves as he rounds the corner.

"Hey," Toby nods.

"Smells great in here," Ian comments, sitting at the table, not even offering to help. Toby recognizes that there really isn't much to help with at this point, but it still irks him that Ian doesn't even think of it.

"I grilled burgers," Clara says, turning from the counter to bring a plate of toppings to the table.

"I chopped the onions," Toby announces proudly, and Clara smacks his shoulder.

"Well I closed a 3.2 million dollar account today, so I guess we're all winners," Ian responds smugly. Toby has to physically force his eyes not to roll.

"That's exciting," Clara says, rubbing his shoulder. "Have you almost met your investor goals?"

"Getting close. Very close," Ian says emphatically as he squirts mayonnaise on his bun. "How's work going, Toby?" he asks, reaching for a tomato slice.

"It's going," Toby answers.

"They hired some new servers," Clara adds. "Sounds like one of them is cute," she teases, passing around the plate of burger patties.

Toby shakes his head. "Everyone at work is great. It's a fun team."

Ian snorts and Toby eyes Clara with a raised eyebrow.

"That's not really supposed to be funny," Toby comments, trying to keep his tone light.

"No, sorry, I didn't think it was funny," Ian says, smashing his buns together and taking a massive bite. Toby finishes stacking the pickles on top of his onions, then stands up to refill his water glass.

With his mouth still full, Ian continues, "I just have to wonder where this is headed."

Clara's eyes widen, shooting an apologetic glance in Toby's direction.

"I mean, you're working at a restaurant, barely able to make ends meet. Sure, it's a fun place to work, but by the time I was your age, I was working for my first hedge fund. It's not like you even need to go back to college if you don't want to, but it seems like you could set your sights a little higher, you know? You're a smart kid, Toby," he finishes, filling his mouth with more burger.

Clara daintily picks at the chips on her plate. Toby sets his water down and settles on his chair.

"Well, thanks for the tips, Ian," he says blandly and takes a bite. The burger is seasoned perfectly and the combination of flavors helps to lessen the sting of the previous comments. Slightly.

"What?" Ian says, noticing Clara's body language for the first time. "Do you think I'm wrong? Clara, I know we're on the same page here."

Toby looks at his sister questioningly.

"Ian, I just don't think this is—"

"Clara, you can't keep babying him. He's a big boy. And someone needs to say it how it is," Ian asserts, continuing to eat between accusations.

"You know, I think I'll just take my food to go," Toby says, picking up his plate. "I'll bring this back to you when we do brunch with Dad and Carole," he says, motioning to the plate and standing up. "Thanks for dinner, Clara."

"Toby, wait—" she calls after him, but he closes the door without looking back.

CHAPTER 23

After finishing a lunch shift for a change, Toby begins the short walk home. With the sun shining and his conversation with Abby fresh on his mind, he can't help but grin.

"Want to come with?" she had asked after telling him about a local band that was playing the next weekend in the Pearl. Surprising even himself, he had said yes. Was this his first official social outing since moving here? Well, besides Bunco. His fingers tingle just thinking about it. Maybe he has been missing spending time with friends.

Toby stops mid-stride when he sees it. An unfamiliar car parked in front of his walkway, practically screaming 'rental' with a new paint job and an Arizona license plate. Why? Why couldn't they have gone to Clara's first? He sighs, trudging toward the back of the vehicle.

The front car doors open simultaneously as he approaches.

"Toby!" his dad practically shouts, reaching out to him with open arms. Even as an adult, being embraced like this still makes him feel about nine years old.

"Hey Toby," Carole adds with bland affect, moving toward him around the front of the car in a freshly pressed pantsuit. Did she really travel like that? Toby can't help but think it couldn't have been comfortable on an airplane. Though, they probably traveled first class. As he leans down to hug her, his curls land in her face, causing her nose to wrinkle in distaste.

"I thought you'd be over at Clara's first," Toby comments, stepping back and shoving his hands in his pockets protectively.

"We got in a little early and thought we'd try to catch you before your shift tonight," his Dad explains.

"Well," Toby shrugs, "glad it worked out." Momentarily hesitating, he awkwardly grins as they stand facing each other in the street.

"Clark has been so excited to see your new home," Carole nudges.

"Oh, right, sure. Come on in," Toby responds hastily, turning and ushering them up the walk. Locking the car, Clark reaches for Carole's hand and leads her toward the door.

"I don't really have furniture or anything yet," Toby apologizes as they step into the living room.

"That's alright, who needs chairs, right?" Clark says, his voice jovial.

"I mean, I do have one chair, at least," Toby explains, pointing to a half-moon table with a single chair pressed against the far wall.

His Dad laughs, motioning for Carole—still clutching her purse near the door—to join them in the middle of the somewhat empty room. A large bean-bag chair sits beneath the front window, but neither Clark nor Carole move to make themselves at home. Carole, turning a degree to the left, allows her eyes to wander over the blank walls while avoiding eye contact with Toby.

"So, this is it," Clark says, taking it in.

"Yep, this is it," Toby sighs.

"What made you want to live over here instead of near Clara?"

"Ummm, mostly because of the walkability of the neighborhood. I figured it would be easier since..." Toby hesitates, "...uh, since I don't have a car...right now," he finishes.

Clark grunts. "Right."

Toby drops his eyes to the floor, tucking a curl behind his ear. "So how's the practice going?" he asks, hoping to change the subject.

"Never been busier," Carole answers and Clark turns to her, pleasantly surprised.

"Never been busier," Clark repeats, a tender expression on his face. Carole's cheeks turn pink, and she turns back to her wall watching.

Toby, not quite sure how to interpret that interaction, clears his throat. "Carole, are you still with your real estate company, or—"

"Carole's working at the office now," his Dad cuts in.

"Oh," Toby says, his eyebrows lifting in surprise. That explains it. "How did that come about?"

"One of our staff ended up going to prison for tax evasion and I needed a new gal," Clark answers nonchalantly, winking at Carole.

Toby coughs, desperately suppressing his desire to escape this conversation immediately. Or go tell Jo about it. Tax evasion? 'New gal'? You can't make this stuff up.

"Still working late hours?" he asks, attempting to keep a straight face.

"Always. You know. That's what pays the bills," he says,

clapping Toby on the shoulder. "If I'm not available, patients can always go down the street—"

"—to Dr. Robison, I know, Dad," Toby finishes. Glancing at his phone, he says, "Actually, I need to shower before work. You two are welcome to just hang out, or—"

"No, it's alright, Toby, we'll head over to Clara's. Will we see you tonight after your shift?"

"Depends. If it's dead, I may be able to head out early. Otherwise, we're meeting for brunch tomorrow right?"

"You got it," his Dad answers.

"We're paying," Carole adds, a vacant smile on her lips.

Toby nods, breathing a massive sigh of relief when the door finally closes, then walks down the hall to the bathroom.

"So you told your Dad that you had to shower before work. But now you're here. And your shift doesn't start for over an hour," Jo muses, shuffling out onto the step, her hand carefully gripping the metal railing next to her.

Toby nods, smirking. "I did have to shower before work," he argues, shaking his wet hair as if to emphasize his point.

Jo rolls her eyes. "C'mon in, then."

Toby jumps the few steps up to the door and walks to his regular spot on the couch. Within moments, Precious is purring on his lap.

"I just don't see how they even ended up together. Carole is...kind of missing a personality."

Jo raises her eyebrow.

"No, seriously. It's like nothing is going on in her head. Ever. She says the most random things and the look on her face is like...like...I don't know how to describe it. I'm going to have to introduce you."

"Sounds lovely," Jo quips.

Toby leans back into the couch, sighing and staring at the ceiling. "Maybe I'm being too critical. At least my Dad didn't interrogate me right off the bat. That's progress, right?"

Jo continues to stare at him, her eyes wide.

"What?" Toby asks, sitting upright.

"Schermis lick," Jo slurs, her eyes blinking rapidly.

"Huh?" Toby asks, eyebrows furrowed. As Jo attempts to speak again, the right side of her mouth droops slightly—not moving with the rest of her mouth. Toby stares, attempting to process the strange behavior when something clicks. Quickly jumping from his seat, he darts into the kitchen, knocking over a tv stand that had been propped against the wall, and grabs for the handheld telephone resting on the counter. With shaking fingers, he frantically forces the plastic buttons down in order: 9-1-1.

CHAPTER 24

"Toby," Clara breathes as she sweeps through the automatic doors of the emergency waiting room. Clark and Carole had dropped her at the entrance before searching for a suitable parking space. As they were driving in the evening traffic to reach the hospital, Clara hadn't been able to keep her hands from fidgeting. Navigating the construction in the industrial area before the hospital entrance had seemed interminably long—each stop sign maddeningly redundant. They likely dropped her at the doors just to end the anxiety produced by her constant knee bouncing. Regardless, she is grateful to finally sit next to her brother in the far corner of the room.

"Toby," she says gently, wrapping an arm around his shoulders, her jacket crinkling loudly at the contact.

"Hey," he breathes, lifting his face out of his hands to acknowledge her. His eyes carry a sadness and a maturity that she hasn't witnessed in him before. Her heart twinges.

"Where are things at?"

"Not sure," he answers. "Nobody has given me an update in over an hour."

"What happened?" she asks, then rushes to clarify, "I mean, I understand what happened, but how did you find her?"

Leaning back in the plastic chair, Toby takes a deep breath. "I stopped over there after Dad and Carole came over. I was on my way to work and just...wanted to vent, I guess."

"About Dad and Carole?"

Toby nods. "It wasn't a big deal or anything. I hadn't seen her and...then I was talking and all of a sudden she just started acting really strange. Her face seemed to drop on one side and I couldn't understand her. That's when I called the ambulance."

"Well it's a good thing you were there. Could you imagine?"

"I know, I've been playing that scenario out in my head over and over. She would have just died, Clara. Alone in her apartment. Who knows when I would have noticed—"

"You would have noticed, Tob, you see her almost every day," Clara assures him, patting his knee in an attempt to be comforting.

"Still."

"There's Dad and Carole," Clara says, craning her neck and watching them walk through the doors. They scan the waiting room and she lifts her arm, giving a small wave to catch their attention.

"They came?" Toby asks, not able to conceal his distaste.

"Of course they came."

"I'm not really in the mood to be amicable," Toby complains and Clara flashes her eyes.

"I don't think anyone expects you to be. But I promise I'll mitigate as needed," she says, standing. "Found a parking spot?" Clara asks, turning her attention to the couple as they approach.

"That we did," Clark answers. "Any news?"

Clara shakes her head.

"Did you have to skip your shift to come over here?" he asks Toby.

"Does that matter?" Toby asks and immediately Clara stiffens.

"I'm sure your boss understands," she jumps in.

"No, I'm sure he does," Clark agrees, "I was just worried—since it's such a new job and all that," he says, sitting down across from Clara. Carole takes the seat next to him, setting her purse on her lap.

"I'm going to go get a drink," Toby announces, standing suddenly and walking toward the hall.

"Well he's wound tight," Clark comments, putting an arm around Carole's shoulders.

"Dad, he literally just rode in an ambulance and watched Jo have a stroke," Clara responds, exasperated.

"I know, I know," he breathes, pursing his lips.

"What?" Clara asks.

Clark looks at her innocently, shrugging his shoulders.

"I know that look, Dad. What is it?"

"Nothing!" he insists, and Clara rolls her eyes. "I know why he felt he needed to come..." he starts again, and Clara lets her breath out in a huff.

"But?" she interjects.

Glancing at Carole, he continues. "But he's only had this job for what, a month or so? It's not like being here is actually accomplishing anything. He could have gone to work and then stopped over after." Checking his watch, he says, "His shift would have likely almost been over by now."

"Dad, I don't think—" she starts, but then pauses when she sees Toby winding his way back through the maze of chairs. "Just keep those opinions to yourself, okay? He's had a rough day."

Clark nods and Carole smiles vapidly, digging in her purse for chapstick.

Toby slumps back in the chair, noisily opening a package of mini Oreos, meeting his Dad's eyes as if daring him to comment. He pops a few in his mouth and chews.

"I'm sorry to ruin your night," Toby says after swallowing, black flecks still visible between his teeth.

"You didn't ruin anything," Clara assures him, rubbing his shoulder.

"What were you all up to before you came?" Toby asks, attempting to lighten the mood.

"Nothing much," Clark answers, shifting his weight in the chair. "Just settling in at Clara's."

"I was hanging up my blouses," Carole adds, staring at the wall.

"How long are you staying?" Toby asks.

"Until Tuesday," Clark answers. "That is, if we don't drive Clara crazy before then."

"You won't drive me crazy," Clara says, a small smile on her lips. "Besides, you'll mostly be entertaining yourselves while I'm working. I'm sorry your first few days here landed on such a busy time."

"Nonsense," Clark waves her off. "You do what you need to do. Carole and I will do some sight-seeing."

Before Toby has time to ruminate on this response, he hears Jo's name called above the waiting room chatter. Standing, he walks toward the nurse positioned near the intake desk. Clara watches their conversation, attempting to interpret his body language. Eventually he nods and walks back to their little group.

"She's stabilized," he announces. "Not completely out of the woods yet, but she's comfortable and sleeping. Sounds like tomorrow morning will be the soonest they'll allow visitors."

Clara breathes a sigh of relief. "So happy to hear that. Can we take you home?"

Toby nods, shoving his hands in his back pockets.

"Don't forget these," Clark says, grabbing his half-eaten packet of Oreos from his chair and handing it to him.

"Thanks," Toby chuckles. Clara wraps an arm around his waist as the four of them move toward the exit.

CHAPTER 25

"Didn't they just bring you jello?" Toby teases as Jo presses the red button on her chair for the fourth time since he arrived an hour before.

Jo rolls her eyes. She still isn't talking much, but with the amount of energy she has to exert to form words correctly, it's understandable.

"Are you going to get lemon or cherry this time?" he goads good-humoredly.

She raises her eyebrow, but a nurse enters the room, preventing her from attempting to defend herself.

"Hey Jo, what can I do for you?" she sighs as she straightens the papers on the shelf below the mirror, deep shadows weighing heavy under her eyes.

Jo motions to the bathroom and the nurse nods.

"Sure, let me help you."

As he watches the woman position herself next to Jo and support her as she swings her legs from the bed, Toby can't help but feel a little sheepish. She knew he was teasing, right? He turns his attention back to the television, pretending to be engrossed in a life insurance commercial. As the door shuts to the bathroom, he pulls out his phone.

Swiping open a message from Clara, he reads.

>Dad and Carole want to come to Bob's tonight. You're working dinner, right?

He types: *Yep. Shift starts at 5*

His finger hesitates over his social media apps, but he closes his phone and slips it back in his pocket. Ever since moving to Portland, his desire to keep in touch with old friends has been waning. Each time he had previously logged on, it was an unending feed of announcements. New jobs, marriage proposals, exotic travel—all of which made Toby feel even more inadequate. And it definitely made anything in his life seem unworthy of sharing.

Over the last few days, spending time with his Dad and Carole has been surprisingly manageable. Even enjoyable at times. Surprisingly, not a word has been said about his lack of trajectory or life plan. Clara likely has something to do with that, but regardless, he's grateful.

The door to the bathroom opens and Jo dodders toward the bed with the nurse gripping her arm. Though it takes her a moment, she eventually settles on the bed, adjusting her gown as the nurse slides her table back into place over her lap.

"So you are her neighbor?" the nurse asks, stifling a yawn.

"Yep," Toby nods. "Have you been up all night?"

She nods.

"I'm sorry, that's tough," he comments.

"Ah, it's normal. I'm off in an hour and then I don't work until Friday night."

"Must be tough to switch between days and nights like that."

"Sometimes. If I didn't have kids, I could just be nocturnal," she laughs. "Seriously, though. It's pretty great that you're here. I don't know many young adults who are that invested in their elderly neighbor's welfare."

Toby tucks a curl behind his ear. "Well, not everyone lives next to Jo."

Out of the corner of his eye, he notices a small smile tug at Jo's lips. Not wanting to draw attention to her, Toby waves to the nurse and returns his gaze to the television.

"What do you think is going to happen today? Is Brady going to finally slip up?"

Jo shrugs, reaching for her plastic water cup, taking a sip from the bendy straw. Toby pulls the other chair up and rests his feet, settling back for the third *Days* episode he's watched with Jo in her hospital bed so far.

CHAPTER 26

"How are you holding up?" Clark asks his son, clapping a strong hand on his shoulder.

"I'm tired, but good," Toby answers honestly. "We should know by tomorrow if she's able to be released from the hospital."

"Well I'm glad we were able to make this work before we head home."

"Me too," Toby says sincerely. With bouncing between work and the hospital, he hadn't been able to do as much with them as he'd hoped. Though, if he's honest with himself, it was also a bit of a relief to be able to focus on concrete tasks instead of less tangible relationships. For days, Clara had been updating him on their whereabouts in case it worked out for him to join them, but so far, nothing really jumped out as being too exciting to miss. Guilt niggles at him slightly at being so flippant, but he brushes it off. He's here with them now and that's all that matters.

"How did you hear about this place?" Toby asks.

"Ian told me about it," Clara answers. "Apparently they

often stop here after work, but he said the lunch menu is also fantastic."

"It doesn't look too expensive," Carole says, scanning the prices.

"Nope, very reasonable," Clara responds, "and don't feel like you need to pay today. I can pay for myself and cover Tob—"

"I've got it, Clara," Toby offers. "I've been working a lot lately."

Clara nods, then turns to address the waiter they are following into the rustic dining space. She marvels at a wall of old windows, suspended from the ceiling one on top of another. Though the room is open, the textures and colors all around them somehow make it feel cozy and warm. She takes off her jacket and hangs it on the rack closest to their table.

"So what time is your flight, Dad?" Clara asks, pulling out her chair.

"Ten o'clock. We need to be at the airport around eight. That'll give us time to return the rental."

"Then it's back to patients tomorrow?" Toby questions.

"Back to the grind," his dad agrees.

"It's nice that Carole works with you now," Clara comments. "Seems like you would see a lot more of each other that way."

"If you call waving at each other in the hall 'seeing each other'," Clark laughs and Carole smiles widely.

"Sometimes we eat lunch together for ten minutes in the office," Carole adds.

"How romantic, Dad," Clara teases.

"Hey, it's better than nothing," he retorts, and Toby holds his tongue.

A waitress approaches their table and informs them of the

daily specials. Anything Italian sounds especially abhorrent to Toby after his increased hours at Bob's, so he orders the Eggs Benedict and a side of bacon. He watches Carole hanging on his dad's arm as he orders, then grimaces when she asks Clark to order for her as well. What in the world does he see in her?

Suddenly, something clicks. Carole seems to be completely satisfied with deferring to his judgement in nearly every area. Is that actually all he wants in a partner? In *all* of his relationships? Someone to control? It would definitely explain why things didn't end well in his first marriage. Though, Toby wasn't old enough when they split to really remember much. He pulls the paper off of his straw and takes a drink of water. Something to think about.

"How did everything work out with that patient the other day, Clara?" Clark asks, spreading his napkin across his lap and reaching for his water glass. Toby looks at his sister with curiosity.

"It turned out fine," Clara answers. "The complaint that was filed against her ended up being withdrawn. I spoke with the neighbors and they legitimately had no clue that they had a neighbor with such severe mental health issues."

"So they aren't requiring her to be admitted?" her dad asks in surprise.

Clara shakes her head. "They can't yet. She hasn't reached the point where it's considered medically necessary."

"But if it's a safety concern—"

"They don't think it's that yet either. I know," she says, taking in his expression, "it seems ridiculous, but her insurance won't cover it unless one of those two things is officially noted."

Clark breathes heavily. "That wouldn't happen in Minnesota."

"Dad, you don't really work with patients like this," Clara argues.

"Well I have colleagues that do," he asserts. Clara backs off, taking a sip of her water as a distraction.

"Do you two have any other trips planned for the year?" Toby cuts in, returning a grateful smile from Clara.

"We're going to Mexico in June," Carole answers excitedly.

"Well, that's more of a work trip. I'm going to a workshop down there."

"In Mexico?" Toby asks skeptically.

"It's for pharmaceuticals," Carole announces proudly.

"Not really," Clark says in a patronizing tone, patting her knee. Toby shoots Clara a sidelong glance as he adjusts his glasses.

"Toby, where do you see yourself in five years?" Clark asks and Toby's heart immediately starts to race. We were doing so well, he laments silently. How can he answer that honestly in a satisfactory way? He has literally no idea where he'll be in five years, and Clark knows it. Normally, in a situation like this, he would give his dad the answer he was seeking. Somehow, though both of them recognize that his answer doesn't hold water, it avoids the conflict and allows his dad to continue living in a false reality where his son is stepping in line. But what's the point? This time...he simply can't bring himself to play the game.

"I honestly have no idea, Dad," he admits, not meeting his eyes. "My goal is to work and just try a bunch of different things to see if something clicks. I'm also planning to do a lot of reading—"

"So your plan is to read?" Clark interrupts skeptically. "What do you think you're going to find? Some magical get rich quick scheme?"

Toby remains silent, obviously hurt by the comment.

"Dad," Clara starts, but is quickly cut off.

"I'm honestly trying to understand you, Toby," Clark

continues. “Don’t you see that most of your peers are already graduating or making six figures?”

Toby stares, swallowing hard. Not pulling any punches, is he.

“Yeah, Dad. I see it. But what do you want from me? I’m doing everything I can to find my path. It’s not like I didn’t try to do things your way.”

“My way? Toby, there isn’t any ‘my way’, there is ‘the way’. If you don’t get an education, you’re going to make less money.”

“But what if my goal isn’t just to make money? I don’t need a fancy house or a fancy car. I just want to find something that will allow me to live comfortably and to be happy.”

“Are you planning to have a family at some point?”

“I don’t know, maybe?” Toby answers, throwing up his hands in exasperation.

“Well you’ll recognize the value of a good living if that happens, but by then it will be too late,” he warns. “Toby, I’m not trying to control you, but I’ve lived through this. I know how to be successful—”

“In all the wrong things!” Toby asserts, keeping his voice purposefully low, attempting not to make a scene. Clara twists her napkin uncomfortably.

“You weren’t successful in your marriage and you weren’t around, Dad. I’m more than grateful for your hard work and the luxuries that you provided, but working all hours...was that really worth it?”

Clark purses his lips as Carole rubs his arm. “I don’t think you really understand.”

“I think we should agree to disagree,” Toby says softly. “You can live your life and I can live mine.”

Next to their table, the waitress appears with a tray full of food. She carefully places each plate in front of them and they thank her. Toby shoves a forkful of food in his mouth, barely tasting it, as angry tears sting the corners of his eyes.

"WHY DID YOU GO THERE?" Clara asks, her voice low, standing next to Toby in the parking lot as Clark and Carole drive away.

"Me? You're asking why I—" Toby stops short. "Are you kidding, Clar?"

"No, you didn't need to accuse—"

"Clara, Dad constantly attacks my life choices. We were sitting there having a nice conversation and then, out of nowhere—" he shakes his head. "I have tried just sitting back and listening. I have tried giving him the answers he wants. Nothing works! Sure, it avoids conflict in the moment, but then it comes up again, and again. I need him to know that we see things differently," Toby explains, his hands gesticulating. "Maybe then he'll lay off."

Clara sighs. "He's just worried about you Toby. There's a lot of risk in what you're doing—"

Toby groans, running his hands through his hair. "Again with the risk," he groans. "Risk of what, Clara? Risk of not being rich?"

"How about being homeless? What would you have done if you couldn't have crashed at my place? You criticize us, but our stability is what has allowed you to even have the flexibility to explore different options! What if we weren't around, Toby?" Clara demands.

"Then I would have figured something else out!" Toby argues, staring at her intently. Clara spins on her heel, her short hair whipping into the air, and stomps in what Toby can only assume is the direction of her car. He moves as if to call out to her, but nothing leaves his lips. She doesn't meet his eyes as she pulls out and drives directly past him to the exit.

AFTER ARRIVING HOME in Jo's Buick, Toby stares forlornly at his front door. Tapping his fingers on his jeans pocket, he turns and strolls down the hill, unwilling to sit stewing alone in his townhome for the time being. At least getting some fresh air has the potential to lower his frustration levels.

He wanders the streets of his neighborhood somewhat aimlessly, turning randomly without any thought of a potential destination. With every step, the tension in his chest seems to decrease, and eventually, he begins to tread lightly on the concrete instead of punishing it with every step. Rounding another corner, his attention is drawn to a small park with a duck pond. How had he never noticed that this existed before? True, he hadn't necessarily made an effort to explore the side-streets before this very moment, but it seems odd that he wouldn't have noticed a body of water close by on his Google maps.

As his feet leave the sidewalk and connect with the dirt path, the sunlight is partially obscured by tall trees lining the walkway. The humidity in the air rises and Toby breathes deep. Noticing an empty bench, he walks toward it and sits to observe the mallard swimming peacefully amidst the rushes, leaving gentle ripples in his wake.

A wave of guilt and sadness washes over him at the realization that his father would be boarding an airplane in a few hours and the last words he had said to him were less than kind. Frustration builds within him. I have tried so hard to avoid these types of confrontations, he thinks, angry tears springing to his eyes, but it doesn't matter! It always ends up like this. Dad can't help but spew his opinions and I apparently can't help but get defensive. Leaning back and stretching his legs out, he rests his head on the back of the bench and closes his eyes, wiping them hastily.

What if I'm defensive because I'm worried, too. This thought seems to stop even the air around him. He breathes slowly, the idea sinking in. I'm worried that I made a huge mistake, Toby realizes. That Dad's right. What if this doesn't work out? What if I do end up with no income, no opportunities for a steady job—or worse, find someone that I want to start a life with and have to admit—

"Toby?"

The voice startles him and he bolts upright, scanning for its owner.

"I'm sorry, I didn't mean to scare you," Abby says, her cheeks slightly flushed.

Attempting to calm his heart rate and pull himself together, Toby slides back to the bench, forcing a grin and stealthily wiping his eyes.

"Hey, no worries. I was kind of...in the zone," he chuckles, and she tentatively moves around the bench, sitting next to him. Her dark hair is striking against the greenery and Toby notices for the first time a small, glittery gem in her nose. She smoothes her skirt and crosses her legs, setting her purse on the pine needles.

"You look nice," he comments.

"Oh, thanks. I just got off my shift," she says, waving his comment off. "I smell like…cooking oil."

Toby laughs. "You wore a skirt?"

"Hey, sometimes I get sick of wearing the same pair of black dress pants, okay?" she jests, pretending to be offended.

"No judgment here," Toby says, holding up his hands. "I said you look nice, remember?"

She gives him a sidelong glance, keeping her attention trained on the duck.

"Do you live around here?" Toby asks, suddenly wondering how she ended up at the park after work.

She points through the trees. "My parents live right over there," she explains. "I'm staying with them for a while, just until I can get back on my feet."

Toby nods. "I'm realizing right at this very moment that I don't know much about you."

"Well we've only overlapped shifts, what, like twice?" she says, letting him off the hook.

"I guess that's true," he laughs. "So give me your life in a nutshell."

"My whole life?"

Toby nods.

"Wow, okay...well, I've lived my whole life here. I grew up in this same house, actually. My parents are amazing—obviously, since they're letting me live with them—I graduated high school a year and a half ago and...I still have no idea what I want to do. I moved to Seattle for a bit, but that didn't really work out."

"For school?"

"Boyfriend," she admits sheepishly. "I have two younger brothers that are annoyingly up in my business, but," Abby sighs, "I still love them. Pretty boring, right?"

"No," Toby shakes his head. "It sounds pretty great, actually."

"Yeah, I guess," she muses, staring into the trees. "But sometimes…" she hesitates. "I don't know, it's kind of unrealistic, but sometimes I just want something out of the ordinary. Some exciting thing to just pluck me up and take me somewhere I wasn't expecting. I thought that's what Seattle was going to be. Moving in with someone, new city, all that."

"It wasn't?"

"Well, at first it was amazing, but then...he wasn't

awesome and, it turns out, bills have to be paid no matter where you live," she laughs.

Toby nods, "I hear you there," he commiserates.

"What if I end up forty and I'm still just a waitress at Bob's. You know?" she says, finally turning. "Sorry, that probably wasn't the answer you were expecting," she apologizes, looking at her hands.

"No," Toby jumps in, "it's actually a better answer than I was expecting."

Abby grins, then reaches for her purse, tucking her hair behind her ear. "I better get home," she says, standing. "I guess I'll see you at work?"

"I'm sure we'll overlap, like, twice again sometime," he teases, and she laughs. As he watches her go, he pulls out his phone and begins typing.

CHAPTER 27

"If she recognizes me..." Clara starts, resting her head against the seat of the Buick.

"Then what?" Toby laughs. "Do you think she's going to throw you out?"

"Maybe," Clara says anxiously.

"Here's the deal. Pull your hair up. If she still recognizes you, I'm not claiming you as my sister. I'll just say I found you out in the hallway."

"Thanks, that's helpful."

"No, but seriously," Toby continues. "I don't want her to think that I have some weird connection with Simply Living," Toby explains.

"But you do..." she says, raising an eyebrow.

"Not really," he comments, pulling into a parking spot directly in front of the entrance. Turning off the car, he takes a deep breath. "She's probably going to be out of sorts. The nurse I talked with said she still has moments where she has trouble speaking or focusing."

"The fact that she's functional at all is kind of a miracle,"

Clara comments. "Strokes at eighty-seven…not really something most people recover from."

Toby nods, opening his door.

"Toby," Clara calls, and he sits back in his seat, looking at his sister. "I'm really sorry about the other day."

"It's okay," he says, shrugging it off.

"No, it's not. I still don't think you should've talked to Dad like that—I know, let me finish," Clara insists as Toby begins to protest. "I don't think getting your point across is really going to change anything. Dad thinks the way he thinks and until he sees evidence that your way of doing things works, he's not going to shift his opinion."

Toby sighs, recognizing truth in her statement. "So what do I do then? I always go into our visits with every intention of avoiding conflict, but then he goes off like that and—"

"I know, I would have a really hard time staying silent in that situation, as well. When he started criticizing the way I deal with patients...I don't know how that one would've gone had you not jumped in."

"You're welcome," Toby says.

Clara rolls her eyes. "But," she continues, "I think you need to start viewing it differently. What if every time Dad started criticizing, you reminded yourself that it's his way of showing love? If you just stopped listening to the actual words coming out of his mouth and made up your own internal dialogue?"

Toby nods. "It's worth trying. And I'd be happy to stop listening to the words coming out of his mouth," he chuckles and Clara swats his arm.

"Clar, it's true what you said," Toby continues. "Without you, I wouldn't—"

"No, Toby, I know you would've figured something else out. I think...we just need to trust each other more. We're both pretty smart and capable. There's no reason why we can't both be successful, even if we choose different paths."

Looking down, Toby hesitates.

"You okay?" Clara asks.

"It's just...what if I'm not? What if these feelings I have—or I guess this drive to do things differently—doesn't work out? I don't know where I'm headed Clara. I think that's why I get so defensive."

Clara takes a deep breath. "Toby, none of us really knows. We just assume it will work because we've seen other people find success this way. It's a safe choice, but when you really think about it, any number of things could change in the world to make what I'm doing risky. So maybe...maybe we all just need to recognize that there aren't really any 'safe' choices."

"That actually makes me feel a little better," Toby admits. "Thanks."

"I'll try to do better," Clara says.

"Me too," he agrees, reaching out to give her a side-hug. "Wait, was this just a distraction to avoid going inside to see Jo?"

"Busted," Clara laughs.

"Uh-huh, nice try," Toby says, stepping out of the car. Clara, typically confident and in charge, lags slightly behind him as he walks toward the sliding glass doors. Entering the facility, his shoulders immediately tense. The low ceilings almost make the hallway feel claustrophobic, and any attempts to make the waiting area seem cozy—a few scattered arm chairs, a coffee machine, planters with silk flowers—vastly miss the mark.

"I'm looking for Jo—" he stops short, his mind blanking on her last name.

"Jo Schow," Clara says, moving to the counter next to him. He smiles gratefully.

"You'll need to sign in here," the attendant instructs, motioning to a clipboard. "Her room is 301."

Toby picks up a pen and quickly fills out the form, then slides it to Clara who follows suit. Without thinking to ask for directions, Toby starts down the hall.

"Do you know where you're going?" she asks.

"To room 301," he states confidently, scanning the doors.

"You're so stubborn," Clara says, shaking her head.

"Look, it's right there," he says, puffing out his chest and grinning.

The door ahead of them is slightly ajar, but Toby still knocks before entering.

"Who is it?" Jo calls from inside.

"Hey Jo, it's me, Toby," he says, a smile involuntarily creeping onto his face.

"Toby?" she asks. Not wanting to have this conversation in the hallway, Toby opens the door and walks in. As soon as she sees his face, she lights up.

"Hey," he greets her, sitting on the edge of the bed. While the blankets are more brightly colored, and the bed is somehow closer in design to a real bed, the room still feels very much like a hospital. Sterile and cold.

"Are they taking good care of you?"

"Where's Precious?" she asks, her eyes wide.

"She's doing great, you don't need to worry about her. I've been making sure she gets her breakfast and dinner. I'm sure she misses you, though."

Jo breathes an audible sigh of relief. Suddenly, Toby realizes he left Clara standing in the hall.

"Hey," he says excitedly, "I've got someone I want you to meet." Standing, he walks to the door and ushers Clara in. Jo cocks her head and assesses her for a moment, but doesn't say anything.

"This is Clara," Toby says, "she's my sister."

Jo pushes her glasses up her nose and peers at Clara. "The one who lives here?"

"Yep, the one who lives here. She's my only sister, actually," he chuckles. "I just had to bring her to meet you."

"He talks about you all the time," Clara says, her voice slightly higher pitched than normal.

"Only good things," Jo says slowly, raising her eyebrows at Toby.

"What else would there be to tell?" he teases. "What are you watching?"

"I don't know, really anything to pass the time," Jo answers, picking up the remote and turning off the TV. Though her speech is still slightly slurred, she is easily understandable and obviously more willing to express her thoughts.

"Do you want to go on a walk?" Toby asks, noticing the wheelchair in the corner.

"Is that allowed?" Clara asks worriedly.

"Better to ask forgiveness than permission, right?" Toby says, looking at Jo for approval.

"A walk sounds glorious," she agrees, pushing off her blankets.

Nobody even attempts to stop them as they navigate the halls to the back entrance. Upon exiting the building, neither Clara nor Toby can find any sort of path, so they opt for the sidewalk, hoping that the street won't be too busy this time of day. Jo pulls the thin blanket around her chest. Though the weather is moderate, the humidity outdoors adds an element of chill she hasn't been exposed to for weeks.

"So how's the food here?" Toby asks.

"Abysmal," she retorts.

"As I'd expect," he answers. "Sorry about that, though. Do

you want me to bring you anything next time I come?"

Jo looks at him, her eyebrows furrowed. "How long do you think I'm going to be in here?"

Toby ponders this for a moment. "I wish I had a good answer," he says finally. "But I think it really depends on your physical therapy. If you improve quickly, it shouldn't take too long to get you home. So work hard," he says, patting her shoulder.

Walking in silence, Toby breathes in the air deeply, hoping that it will be as therapeutic for Jo as it is for him.

"Clara," Jo says eventually, "are you older or younger than Toby?"

"Older," Clara laughs nervously.

"Is it not obvious?" Toby jokes. "She even looks more mature and responsible than I do."

"I didn't want to assume," Jo mutters. "You two are close?"

"I think so," Toby answers, looking to Clara for verification. "We have our moments, just like any family."

"We try," Clara teases.

"Clara has an internship at Nike," Toby explains. "She's going to run the company someday."

"That's not really how it works, Tob," Clara laughs. "I'm literally the bottom man on the bottom totem-pole of the Global Communications team."

"She is going to rise up the totem-poles and run the Global Communications team!" Toby announces, spinning Jo's chair in a circle as they pass over a driveway.

"Again," Clara laughs, "not how it works. But thanks for the vote of confidence."

Though they can't see it, a small smile lifts one corner of Jo's lips. Looking straight ahead, she wonders what it would have been like to have a sibling to tease.

"You're lucky to have each other," she concludes, pulling the blanket to her neck as they round another corner.

CHAPTER 28

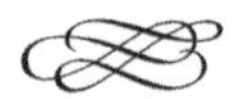

Toby stares at his laptop screen, completely engrossed. His dinner shift overlapped with Abby's tonight and, though they didn't get much time to chat, he did hear her mention this movie to another server in passing. Watching her face light up as she described it while typing in an order made him curious. He'd never heard of it before. Upon arriving home, he searched it and ended up impulse-buying it on Amazon. Halfway through, he is in complete agreement with Abby's assessment.

It occurred to him as he pressed play that he should have invited her over to watch with him. But would that have been weird? He would have had to admit that he was listening to her conversation. But it's not like she was speaking quietly...

A knock on the door startles him and he lazily leans over the beanbag chair to look through the blinds. Seeing Clara waiting on his step, he quickly stands to let her in.

"What are you doing here so late?" he asks, quickly checking for any signs of distress. Her cheeks are flushed and her eyes are shining. She lifts her left hand in front of her face and he sees it. A gleaming golden ring with a glimmering stone in the center.

Toby's eyes grow wide. "What—? How did—when?" he stammers. Clara laughs and bends in half as if she just can't handle her excited energy in an upright position.

"Come in," he says, ushering her through the door.

"Can you believe it?" she says, practically skipping into the living room. "He took me to Paley's,"

"Wow, swanky."

"I know! I've been dying to go," she gushes. "And then with dessert, he got down on one knee—I wasn't expecting it at all." Clara's body is in perpetual motion, touching her ring no less than once every ten seconds or so.

"I—I don't know what to say," Toby admits, tucking his curls behind his ears. "I had no idea you guys were that serious."

"Well we've been dating for almost a year, Tob," she argues.

"Has it been that long? I thought it was months—"

"Ten months, close enough."

"Yeah, no, for sure," he says, taking a deep breath.

"Are you not excited for me?" she asks, her hands on her hips.

"No! Of course I'm excited for you," he assures her, sitting on the edge of the kitchen table.

"You aren't really acting like it," she says, deflating.

"No, Clara, I'm sorry. It's just a lot to take in. Ian, he's—"

"I know you've never really liked him, but I promise he's a good guy. He works hard, he's dedicated, thoughtful—"

"It doesn't really matter what I think, I'm not the one marrying him," Toby says.

Clara huffs and plops down on the beanbag chair, moving Toby's laptop to the side. "What don't you like about him?" she asks, her tone full of frustration.

"I—Clara, it really doesn't matter."

"But it does! I don't want to get married and have my brother hate my husband."

"I don't hate him—"

"Well what don't you like about him?" she repeats, daring him to ignore the question.

Toby takes a deep breath and walks into the living room sitting down cross-legged on the floor next to her. "You want me to be honest?"

Clara nods, biting her lip.

"Okay, let me see if I can explain…" he starts, searching for words that will be truthful without offending. "It's more the feeling I get from him. Every time he's around, I just feel...on edge. Kind of like how I feel around Dad. Like nothing I do could ever be satisfactory." He pauses, trying to gather his thoughts. "And he's so serious. I don't ever see him having fun, or being excited about...really anything. Except for huge deals at work, but even that doesn't feel like actual joy, more like determined...expectation. If that's a thing?" Toby inspects Clara's face for a reaction.

She stares at her hands in her lap. "I think he's excited about things…" she says softly. "He doesn't show it as openly, maybe?" she says, almost to herself.

"Clara—"

"No, it's okay," she says rising to her feet. "I'm...I'm just going to go," she says, twisting the ring around her finger.

Toby's stomach drops, recognizing the look in her face. That look. It's exactly how he envisions his own face looking after talking with his Dad. Did he create that? Were his comments as destructive to Clara as the criticisms he'd received in the past? Guilt wells up inside him and immediately he wants to take it all back. To just show excitement and keep his big mouth shut. But, at the same time, how can he let Clara go through with this without expressing his feelings on the subject? Do his feelings even matter?

"Clara!" he practically shouts, just as her hand is wrapping around the doorknob. She jumps.

"Please, can we talk about this for a second?" he pleads.

She stares at him, her eyes shiny with tears.

"I think...I think I just did to you what you and Dad do to me. And it's weird," he pauses, "because I don't think I've ever done that before. Is this what it feels like? To be so—" he motions with his hands, attempting to describe his emotions, "so full of conflicting ideas that you can't sort it out? I really am so excited for you, Clar, but I also love you and want you to be happy, and I worry that Ian is too serious—not fun and laid back—and that one day you'll come to me and talk about how you feel stuck and then I would feel terrible about *not* saying something way back when. Does that make sense?" He looks to her, but when she doesn't speak, the words keep pouring out of him. "But now, I'm realizing that I don't have any right to that opinion! I don't know Ian, not really. I only know how he makes me feel, which could be from any number of things. It could be me! It could be my own doubts and insecurities causing that, I don't know! And regardless, if you are excited, I should be excited for you! And trust you—like you said—to be wise enough to consider all of those things. To pay attention to your own thoughts and feelings." He is nearly out of breath and takes a moment to compose himself.

Suddenly, Clara bursts out laughing. Tears stream down her face as she leans against the door, clutching her handbag to her stomach. Toby, worried that he sent her into a fit of hysterics, watches—apoplectic, with wide eyes. When she finally begins to wind down, she throws her purse to the side, wipes her eyes, and stumbles back into the living room, flouncing onto the bean bag dramatically. Her head lolls backward with eyes closed.

Toby, turning to follow her, continues to stand in stunned silence, unsure what to do next.

"Oh Toby," Clara says, her eyes still closed. "That's *exactly* how it feels. You know, I look at you and your choices make me nervous, angry, exhilarated and jealous all at once," she says throwing her right hand into the air to emphasize her point.

"Jealous?" Toby asks, incredulous.

"Yes!" she answers, lifting her head to look at him. "Your choices scare me, but they seem so...free. I've never felt that. I've never been willing to take a risk, to just throw caution and rationality to the wind and leap. I'm jealous of that. And look where it's taken you! True, you may not have savings in the bank, but you were able to build a relationship with a woman who doesn't let anybody in—who I was convinced wasn't capable of letting anyone in. You've made her life significantly better."

Toby can feel the blood rushing to his face. How does one respond to a compliment like that?

Clara groans, throwing her head backward again. "I have a headache," she complains.

"Do you want some Tylenol?" Toby asks, but then realizes he probably didn't refill after he ran out last week. "Actually…I don't know if I have any," he admits.

"No, it's fine. I just need to sleep. Too much excitement for one day."

Toby nods, even though she isn't watching. "I'm sorry I reacted that way, Clar. If you're excited, then I'm excited. No caveats."

She stretches her arms in front of her and sits up straight. "Thanks, Toby," she says, again forcing herself to stand.

"Are you going to make it home okay?" he asks, watching her yawn.

"Yeah, I'll be fine," she says, moving toward him and throwing her arms around his shoulders. "Thanks," she whispers.

"Congrats," he says, squeezing her tightly.

CHAPTER 29

Jo stares at her clock, the tail swaying rhythmically back and forth. Precious purrs next to her on the couch and it's like she never left. Is it possible for a place to feel like home and yet foreign all at once? Last night was her first sleep on the new bed. When she arrived home, Toby walked her into the bedroom and showed her a step-stool he had installed during her absence. He had attached it to the bed—with wide steps and a handrail—so that her chance of falling or losing her balance was minimal. The pillow was like sleeping on air…

A knock on the door pulls her to the present. Flicking the blind open, she sees Toby on the step. Standing takes more effort than usual, but he knows this. She has no doubt he'll be patiently waiting for as long as it takes. She grips the armrest of the sofa and heaves herself forward—first to the edge of the cushion to get her legs under her, then to standing. Slowly, she walks the few steps to the entry.

Placing her right hand on the doorknob, she focuses intently—willing her hand to close around it. Creating just enough force, she turns and opens the door wide.

"Morning," Toby greets her, his hair still slightly damp. His white shirt and bow tie feel out of place on her doorstep, but she is again impressed at how handsome he looks in this getup.

"Ready?" he asks, not mentioning the fact that she's standing behind the door in an old robe.

"I need to get dressed," she says as clearly as possible.

"Take your time. I'm early," he says, turning and sitting in his usual spot on the step. She moves into the bedroom and carefully uses both hands to open the middle drawer of her dresser. Selecting a light purple sweater with a bouquet of daisies on the front, she then moves to the closet for a pair of slacks.

At least fifteen minutes later, Jo arrives at the door again. "I need help," she says softly, and Toby turns.

"What do you need help with?" he asks, hopping up the last step.

"I can't button these," she admits, slightly embarrassed, pointing down at her pants. Her fingers couldn't grip the button with enough force to get it through the hole. She had zipped them as far as she could, but worried that the zipper would fall down throughout their walk without the button to keep the pants securely closed.

"No prob," Toby says, opening the storm door and stepping inside. Quickly, and without judgement, he reaches over and deftly slips the button through the hole. Noticing the wheelchair folded next to the end table, he picks it up and carries it to the walkway.

"Do you need help coming down those steps?" he asks, setting it up and turning back toward her. As much as she hates to admit it, her physical therapy has not yet progressed to the point that she can do stairs on her own. Nodding, she places her hand on the railing and waits for Toby to join her. He takes her arm and places it over his shoulder, then grips her waist and holds her as she takes her first step. Eventually, she reaches the bottom and he guides her to the chair.

As she sits, her heart races. Even the smallest task requires such incredible effort, she thinks, breathing deeply in an attempt to relax. Toby flicks up the wheel brakes and begins the walk to Bob's. He stopped by the day before, insisting that she get out of the house and do something fun. Since she had talked about her favorite Italian place back home, Toby offered to serve her lunch. Her attempts to decline his offer were thwarted and, though she hates to admit it even to herself, she truly has been looking forward to this outing all morning.

The cloudy sky threatens rain, but somehow the air is comfortable—even warmer than usual. Jo watches the birds flit between the tree branches as they head down the hill.

"You know I'm tempted to just let the chair go, right?" Toby admits mischievously. Involuntarily, Jo grips the arm rests, and Toby laughs. "I'm not actually going to!"

"It would be fun," she admits, grinning at the mental image of flying down the sidewalk, her chair jumping curbs and frightening pedestrians. Even moving at a normal speed feels thrilling. All of her walks at the care center were aimless; with no actual destination, there wasn't a good reason to move quickly. This feels purposeful and she loves it.

As they wait at the last crosswalk, she looks longingly at Trader Joe's on the corner.

"Has it been a while?" Toby asks, following her gaze.

Jo nods.

"I could take you right after my shift, if you can last that long here at the restaurant. Otherwise, I can take you home when you're finished with your meal and then we can go later."

"Thank you," she whispers, and Toby feels a pang of

sadness. He misses the Jo that would respond with a snarky comment, or insist she could do it herself even when she couldn't. Will that Jo ever come back fully? The walk sign blinks and Toby pushes her across the street, then turns left to the restaurant.

Once inside, he pushes her to a table by the front window and removes the regular chair so that she can stay in hers.

"I'll just be a moment. I'm going to grab you some bread and a glass of water. Or would you prefer a soda?" he offers.

Jo shakes her head, reaching for her napkin. As Toby walks away, she glances out the window and watches a young mother walking up the street with a baby on her front in a carrier. If only they had those when Cheri was little, she thinks. She watches the woman grip the child's fingers and swing her arms as they walk. The mother's lips move, and Jo imagines her talking about the buildings as they pass, or perhaps explaining colors or other vocabulary words. Just like she used to do...

"This," she had said, kneeling down on the grass, "is a snail." She held it up in front of Cheri, who was crawling around the edge of the playground, the knees of her pants scuffed and threadbare. Cheri immediately noticed the object in her hand and flipped to a sitting position, leaving both hands free.

"Don't squish it," she had instructed. "Gentle, soft." She carefully placed the snail in Cheri's outstretched palm. At first, Cheri had stared at it, immediately beginning to lose interest until...

Her squeal of delight pierced the playground air as the snail emerged, beginning to slowly move across her hand. Thankfully, Jo had the foresight to keep a grip on her hand, preventing the snail from flying into the grass as Cheri's hand jumped in excitement.

"Shhhh," she had said, "just watch quietly."

But no amount of 'shhh'ing had helped. It was simply too exciting to witness such a thing.

"Snail," Jo repeated, pointing at the shell. "Snail."

"Ssssail," Cheri said, attempting to mimic her. Within minutes, though Jo had returned the snail to the wood chips, that's the only word Cheri would say as she continually toddled back to check on the creature.

"Here you go," Toby says, interrupting her reverie. He places a basket of warm bread on the table, then places her glass next to her place setting. "Did you get a chance to look at the menu?"

Jo shakes her head.

"Okay, not a problem. Do you know what you typically like to get? What did you like at that place back in Stillwater?"

She smiles, focusing on forming each word in order. "Meatballs," she eventually gets out. "With spaghetti."

"Well that's easy," Toby says, not even needing to write anything in his notebook. "Do you want any broccoli raab along with that?"

She stares at him blankly.

"It's a green—a vegetable. We cook it in butter and garlic."

Jo's Doctor had suggested that she eat more vegetables. Though she is skeptical, she nods in agreement.

"Alright, sounds great. I hope they live up to expectations," he says, then moves to the computer dock to enter in her order.

Jo looks around the restaurant and notices more people in the dining room. Mostly couples, but a few groups of friends, likely on their lunch break judging by their dress. She twists her napkin in her lap, scanning the tables.

Her stroke had been terrifying, but the thought of never being fully independent again made her want to throw up. Without even eating this time. Her physical therapist had expressed confidence in her ability to build up muscle strength and tone, to strengthen her brain pathways again. But everything seems to be moving so slowly.

Her first night home, she stumbled upon her notebook with all of her notes on Brett. During her hospital stay, she had all but forgotten about it. But, she thinks, as soon as someone showed up at the house again to talk money, she surely would have realized the need to get to the bottom of this. Her stomach drops with a sudden realization. Hospital bills. She shudders, wondering what horrifying number she'll find deducted from her account.

"Alright," Toby says, approaching the table with a steaming plate. He carefully places it in front of her, then sets a shaker with parmesan cheese in the middle of the table. "Bon appetit," he says, with a flourish of his arm.

Jo smiles her half, goofy smile. "Looks wonderful," she says, the aroma of garlic tantalizing her taste buds.

"I wish I could sit with you," he says. "If these other tables slow down, I'll come hang out for a few minutes," he promises, winking. Jo smiles, but is secretly grateful for the alone time. She blinks slowly, attempting to relax her muscles in the hope that the pressure behind her eyes will dissipate. She can't tell if the tension in her neck and shoulders is aftermath of the stroke or simply a result of trying to think faster than her brain seems to be capable of at the moment.

Speaking takes incredible processing power. Not only to physically form the words, but to form a thought that then has to be organized into a coherent sentence, which *then* is formed into words and spoken. For Jo, the right side of her mouth is not the only thing that still seems to be partially sleeping.

Picking up her fork and knife, she takes her time cutting the first meatball into bite-sized pieces. Just from the look of it, she can tell it won't be as good as Victoriano's. Well, she thinks, maybe that judgement is a tad hasty. Twirling the noodles with her fork—bumbling slightly with her left, stronger hand—she finally spears a piece of meatball and concentrates on getting it to her mouth. She chews.

No, definitely not as good as Victoriano's. Texture is wrong, too much oregano, too little parmesan. Not terrible, just not...she pauses mid-chew. What is happening? Pressure builds in her chest and her eyes burn. Is she—is she starting to cry? She quickly swallows and sets her fork on her plate, reaching for her napkin. Tears have begun to well up, held back only by a stiff lower eyelid. Unable to contain the surge in emotion, she gives in and finds herself staring out the window to avoid the attention of other patrons.

Confused at the outburst, she attempts to analyze it while tears stream down her cheeks. Is it possible that she has become unhinged by a meatball? No, she thinks. The nurse said this is a common occurrence after one experiences a stroke. But even so...what if this is simply a magnification of feelings that are real? That do actually exist within me? *Why am I crying over a meatball?* She wipes away the tears pooled at the base of her jaw before they drip to her shirt.

As the worst of it passes, she feels a sense of release. Turning back to her plate, she reaches for her cup—using both hands to bring it to her lips—and takes a sip of water before filling her fork a second time.

The meatball is just a microcosm of my life, she realizes. Something alien that should be familiar. Spending time in the hospital—alone—had definitely made her think. Is that how it's going to be? When I die, I'll be tucked in by a nurse I barely know with a blanket that's not mine and—that's it? Nobody will really miss me, or even know that they should.

"How is it so far?" Toby asks, stopping at her table on his way to deliver drinks to the next booth. Jo nods, grateful that her mouth is full. He moves on, but gives her a quizzical look before doing so. She'll blame it on allergies later.

CHAPTER 30

"I can't believe you sat there for my entire shift," Toby says. "Didn't you get bored?"

Jo shakes her head. "I love watching people," she states simply as they cross the doors onto the sidewalk.

Toby laughs as he pushes the chair across the street. "As promised," he says, taking her to the door of Trader Joe's. "Just tell me which aisles to go down. Will a basket do it?"

Jo nods, and Toby picks one up as they enter through the sliding doors. He takes his cues, obediently pushing her toward the oatmeal, yogurt, frozen foods section, and snacks. Her excitement level seems to increase with each new turn, elated at the idea of having all of her favorites restocked in her pantry and refrigerator. After checking out, Toby places a very full double paper bag on her lap, then pushes her back to the sidewalk.

"You're sure that's not too heavy? If it is...I guess you're out of luck because I can't hold it and push at the same time," he chuckles.

"It's crushing me," Jo says sarcastically, her slight slur making it all the more hilarious.

"Hey! If you're able to tease me that must mean your brain is working well, right?"

They walk in silence for a few blocks, mostly because Toby is breathing heavily from the exertion of pushing the chair, Jo, and the groceries up the hill. When they finally reach level ground, his breathing begins to return to normal. Though it's barely dusk, the air is cool and Jo regrets not having brought a jacket along.

"Jo, can I ask you something?" Toby asks as they approach her walkway. "You seemed a little...out of sorts at the restaurant. Is anything bothering you? Or did I do something wrong?"

He stops near the steps and rounds the chair to talk face to face.

"No," she starts, "you didn't do anything wrong. I think my brain is...all over the place right now," she explains slowly.

"I'm sure," he says, sitting on the steps. "I know it's probably just that. But since you've been home, you seem less happy. Am I making that up? Maybe it's just because your body isn't working the way it used to, so I'm interpreting things in a weird way," he says, standing up and shrugging it off. When he offers her his hand, she doesn't take it. He looks at her with eyebrows furrowed and slowly retracts.

"I want to keep working on our case," she says, and Toby's eyes immediately open wide in shock. "We've lost weeks. Who knows what he's been up to," she says, waving her arm.

"Sure," Toby replies. "I guess I thought you'd forgotten all about that."

"How could I!" She pauses, gathering energy. "If anything, I've been thinking about it more."

Toby waits patiently, recognizing that she's not finished yet.

"I'm going to have bills," she continues with a worried

expression. "And if I don't have my money, I won't be able to pay them," she finishes, taking a deep breath.

"That's...yeah. Definitely," Toby nods.

"Tomorrow?"

"Sure, I just don't know—"

"He should be working Wednesday," she says slowly. "Follow him after his shift? See what he does in the evening?"

Toby nods. "Tomorrow's my day off, so I'm free whenever." A cloud seems to pass over him and he moves to speak, but thinks better of it.

Jo looks at him questioningly.

"I was thinking...would it be alright if I brought Clara along? My sister? I'm not sure if you remember meeting her—"

"I remember. Would she be up for it?" Jo asks, raising her left eyebrow.

"No," Toby admits, tucking a curl behind his ear and laughing at her insinuation. "But that's exactly why I want to invite her."

THE NEXT EVENING, Toby and Jo sit in front of a door at Nike headquarters in Beaverton, waiting for Clara to get in the backseat.

"Is she coming?" Jo asks, clearly perturbed.

"I texted her, she knows we're here," he answers, looking intently at the stream of people going in and out, searching for her.

"What if she didn't see the text?"

Toby opens his phone and turns the screen to face Jo. "My messaging app actually shows me if someone's read the message or not. It's nice—you don't have to worry about whether they saw it or not and inundate them with extra messages."

Jo grunts. "Whatever happened to just walking in and telling her we're here?"

"I'm way too lazy for that," Toby laughs. Suddenly, he sees her. She exits the building, chatting with a man wearing a puffy vest and khakis. He waves and walks toward the bike racks.

As they watch her stride toward them, Jo asks, "Did you tell her what we'd be doing?" She takes in Clara's clean slacks, blouse, scarf, and sleek hair.

"Definitely not," Toby answers.

"That blouse is not going to enjoy hiding in a bush," Jo comments derisively.

Clara opens the door closest to her and hops in. "Hey," she greets them, "sorry I made you wait. I needed to shoot off a message before I forgot."

"No worries," Toby says.

"We might be late now," Jo says under her breath. Toby looks in the rearview mirror. It doesn't seem like Clara heard that last comment.

"So where are we headed?" Clara asks.

Toby sneaks a sidelong glance at Jo. "Ummm," he fills the time, not sure how to answer. "We're going to do something that Jo wants to do."

"Oh yeah? Sounds great. What is it that you like to do, Jo?" Clara asks energetically.

"I think it will be best if it's a surprise," Jo answers, and Toby suppresses a laugh, looking in his side mirror to avoid Clara's gaze.

"Okay," Clara answers hesitantly, a nervous grin on her face.

"How was your day?" Toby asks, attempting to change the subject.

"Good," she says, "I ordered hundreds of bubble tablets today."

"Bubble tablets?" Toby questions.

"Yeah, we thought it would be fun to have a gigantic bubble fight after the 5k," she explains. "Kind of a last minute addition, but I think it's going to be a big hit."

"The event is next Saturday?" Toby asks.

"Yep," she confirms, "and I can't wait."

"For it to be over?" he asks, grinning.

"You got it," she laughs. "I need a break!"

As Toby turns left and begins to drive up the hill, Clara stops, noticing their trajectory, and gasps. "Are we—Toby we're not—"

Jo turns in her seat to look at her. "Not what?" she asks innocently.

Clara, unable to find the words, stares straight ahead. As Toby parks the car a few blocks away, he notices her pursed lips in the back seat.

"Toby, can I have a word," she requests, her voice stern.

"Sure," he says, putting on the parking brake, opening his door, and stepping out into the street. Rounding the back of the car, Clara shuts her door and immediately crosses her arms over her chest and turns to face him.

"Seriously? You brought me on one of your spy missions?" she accuses in an angry whisper.

Toby grins. "Clara, you just told me the other day that you wished you could be more carefree. This is as fly-by-the-seat-of-your-pants as it gets."

She rolls her eyes, turning to survey the street. "So what, we wait until he drives by and then follow him? What if he sees us? Or calls the police?"

"Clara, you've said yourself that this guy is a jerk—"

"Which is exactly why he'd do something like that!"

"We're not going to get close, and depending on where he goes, we can decide whether it makes sense to follow."

Clara puts her hands on her hips and looks the other direction.

"Jo hasn't been the same since she's been back," he says, his voice low, as he moves closer to his sister. "I just want her to be happy again. She's the one who brought this up, I didn't suggest it. Maybe she needs a project—some sort of purpose to wake up to every morning."

"Knitting," Clara whines. "Why couldn't she take up knitting?"

Toby laughs and puts a hand on her shoulder. "I promise I won't let it get out of hand."

"Pretty sure you don't know what 'out of hand' is or we wouldn't be here," she quips, opening the door and sliding back into her seat.

AFTER WAITING for about fifteen minutes, Jo points out the front window. Toby, following her gaze, sees the car. Waiting until the blue Civic reaches a stop light further down the hill, Toby pulls out into the street. He hangs back for Clara's sake, even though there are three cars between him and Brett. Looking in the rearview window, he can barely see his sister. Attempting to obscure herself, she slides down in her seat even further, pulling up the collar of her jacket.

"He's in front of us, Clara," Toby laughs. "He's not going to be looking in the back seat. Besides, Jo is much more recognizable to him than you."

"Not true!" Clara insists in a muffled voice. "We know each other really well."

Toby raises his eyebrows.

"Not like that," Clara says in a disgusted tone, watching Toby's expression in the rearview mirror. "He has gone through some things lately and when our sh—" she pauses, realizing that Jo is listening. Clearing her throat, she continues, "when I would see him around the neighborhood, we would talk about it."

"What a coincidence. He lives near you?" Jo asks, swiveling in her seat to hear better.

"Mmhmmm," Clara answers, her discomfort at being dishonest evident in her face.

"What did you talk about?" Jo questions.

"Umm, lots of things, but especially his divorce last year."

"He's divorced? Seems too young for that," Jo mutters.

"He is young," she agrees. "But he was married for four years and they have a little boy together."

"He has children?" Jo exclaims, horrified.

"Only one, but yes. I don't know much about this girl he's dating, besides the fact that she works at—well, that she works with him."

"Jo thinks they're in cahoots," Toby explains, waiting for Clara's reaction. She purses her lips and tucks her head into her jacket like a turtle.

"When Toby asked to bring you along, I didn't realize we'd be getting insider information. This might be helpful," Jo muses.

"To be fair, Clara didn't know that she'd be giving insider information today either," Toby reminds her. He follows the Civic around another turn and slows down, realizing that the buffer cars are no longer there. Eventually, Brett parks in the driveway of a modest ranch-style home, opens the garage door, and goes inside.

Jo sighs audibly and her shoulders droop. "He's home. That means it could be hours before he comes out again."

"It could be," Toby confirms.

"He may just be home for the rest of the evening," Clara states, "which would be a very *normal* thing to do." She raises an eyebrow and stares Toby down in the mirror.

Resting his elbow on the arm rest, he turns his body

toward Jo. "Well? What do you want to do? I'll wait with you if you want," he offers.

"No," Jo says, deflated. "You both have better things to do than sit outside some guy's house. We'll have to come up with a better plan. Maybe we could look around the property and see—"

"I don't want you to get arrested, Jo, I don't think that's a good idea," Clara jumps in. Then, taking a note from Toby, she adds, "Besides...if he were involved in something illegal, don't you think he'd keep it away from his home base?"

Jo nods, considering this thought. Suddenly, the garage opens again and Brett—now in joggers and a hoodie—walks to his car carrying a shoebox.

Clara perks up. "What was that in his hand?"

"Looks like a small box," Toby says, turning the car back on. "Should we follow?"

"Absolutely," Jo says excitedly, gripping the armrest.

Toby chuckles and puts the car in gear, careful to wait a few seconds before following. As the Civic turns right at the stop sign, Toby pulls up to the intersection and Jo watches down the street to anticipate any quick turns that may be needed.

Eventually joining more traffic, Toby relaxes—not having to worry so much about being seen.

The Civic takes a turn and Clara furrows her brow. "Is he going toward the hospital?"

"Huh," Toby says. "Looks like he's heading that direction."

As the landscape becomes more industrial, Brett turns just before the hospital exit and heads north.

"What could possibly—" Jo says, but then the Civic swerves into a street parking spot, and Toby—seeing one directly ahead—does the same. Jo watches as Brett hops out of his car and begins walking.

"Tob, I think he's walking to the Green," Clara says, but Toby looks at her in confusion.

"Gateway Green. The park with biking trails," she clarifies. "Haven't you been?"

"When would I have done that exactly?" Toby asks, grinning at the absurdity of him driving across town to park on the street and walk to a park. "I don't even own a bike."

"Okay, whatever, it doesn't matter. You're going to lose him!"

Toby's eyes light up. "Are you interested in what's in the box?" he teases his sister.

"Not that—I mean, maybe a little—but seriously! He's already a block and a half away!"

"Jo, I think you may have to stay in the car for this one. Do you feel comfortable with Clara and I—"

"I'm not going!" Clara insists. "If he sees me, we're done."

"He's seen all of us," Toby counters.

"But you only once," Jo points out.

"Okay, good point. Clara, you keep Jo company, I'll go," he says, quickly stepping out to the street and shutting the door behind him.

CHAPTER 31

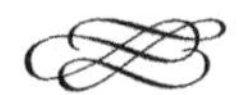

With his hood pulled over his hair—his most memorable feature, by far—Toby follows Brett, staying a block behind him with his phone in hand as a prop. If Brett did happen to look behind him, all he'd see is a guy watching YouTube videos on his way to the Green, or whatever Clara called it.

Eventually, Brett enters the park—still carrying the small shoebox, along with something else that Toby can't quite make out. As Toby follows, he spots Brett down a path to his right. A group of moms with strollers moves up the path and Toby waits for them to pass, then falls in behind them. Brett is in the distance and he still has a clear view.

"I know," the mom in the pink leggings comments. "Potty training is the worst. I'm so glad that our preschool supports that. They're working with him during the day, so all I really have to do is slap a pull-up on him at night and call it good."

The other two women laugh. "I wish we were so lucky. Ours requires that we pull our kid out for a couple of weeks. That's why I'm waiting for summer."

"You're not enrolling for summer?" pink leggings asks.

"Well I have to at least three days a week, but then I'm only missing a few days of childcare, not every day, you know?"

The women nod in agreement. Toby tunes out their chatter as he sees Brett leave the path and walk into the trees. Forcing himself to be patient, he walks along behind the strollers until he reaches his best estimation of where Brett turned. Trying to look inconspicuous, he lifts his phone to his ear and pretends to be on a call. Giving off an air of nonchalance, he saunters to the edge of the small stream and scans the area. Movement catches his eye, and it's all he can do not to immediately turn that direction.

Patiently, he creates a fake conversation and eventually turns. Upstream, he finds Brett using a small trowel to dig a hole in the soft earth. What is he doing? Toby turns again to the stream, allowing himself to glance toward Brett every few minutes. Brett, satisfied with the size of the hole, places the box inside and buries it with the overturned earth. Then, he moves to the stream and rinses off his hands and the trowel, shakes it dry, then turns back to the path.

Toby waits a good five minutes before walking quickly back the way he came. What in the world did he just witness? Could Jo be right about Brett? Is he hiding something? It is only when he reaches the street that he realizes he could have dug up the box and checked its contents, but the very idea makes him feel nauseous. What if it was something dangerous? Or illegal? Not worth the risk, despite the fact that his curiosity is piqued.

Crossing the street, he notices that the blue Civic is gone. He hurriedly walks the block or so to the Buick and sees Clara and Jo chatting away inside.

"Hey," he says, breathless as he opens the door.

"Toby, we were beginning to worry!" Clara says, breathing a sigh of relief.

"I know, sorry," he apologizes, "I had to wait for a bit before coming back."

"Brett left a few minutes ago," Jo says, pushing her glasses up. "Give us the low-down," she commands, her speech still slower than normal.

"The low-down?" Toby laughs. "How do you even know that phrase?"

"I know lots of phrases," Jo insists, crossing her arms.

"Did you hear someone say it at the restaurant the other day?" Toby teases, and Jo rolls her eyes.

"Just tell us what happened," Clara says impatiently.

"Okay," Toby answers, strapping on his seat belt. "I'm not sure exactly what I just witnessed. I followed him up the path a ways and then he turned off into the trees. I followed—pretending I was on the phone, which I think was quite genius—and saw him dig a hole."

Clara's eyebrows furrow. "He dug a hole?"

"Yep. He had a trowel with him, along with the box. He dug a hole and then put the box in it."

"He buried it?" Jo questions.

"That he did," Toby answers, slapping his hands on the wheel at ten and two. Turning on the car, he pulls out into the street and heads toward Clara's house.

"Why would he do that?" Clara asks, slumping against the seat.

"I have no idea. But it is suspect, don't you think?" Toby says.

"It's evidence!" Jo exclaims, making Toby jump with the unexpected energy. "Go dig it up!" she says, reaching for the door handle.

"I thought about that," Toby says, putting a hand on her shoulder before she can exit the vehicle. "But I don't think that's a good idea. What if it *is* evidence?"

"Or what if he comes back and finds us there," Clara whispers.

"You're scared?" Jo asks, her eyes intense.

"Not scared," Toby says, "But I don't want to do something that could get any of us in trouble."

Jo slumps back into her seat.

"We know where it is," Clara offers, "so if we decide we need to see it, we could come back, right?"

In the rearview mirror, Toby sees Clara with wide eyes, pointing at the window and obviously trying to send him a message. Completely oblivious, he shrugs and continues driving.

"We should probably drop Jo off first before we head to my place," Clara says.

"Why?" Toby asks. "We're already—"

"That makes sense," Jo says. "We're closer to our houses than to Clara's neighborhood."

"How do you—" Toby begins in confusion, but Clara cuts him off.

"She's seen Brett's neighborhood and, *since I live close to him*, she can kind of guess whereabouts my house is," she says, sending a meaningful glance to Toby.

"Oooooh, right," Toby says, understanding finally dawning. Changing his direction, he heads toward his house.

After parking and assisting Jo into her living room, Toby returns to the car to drive Clara home.

"That was a close one," he chuckles, and Clara smacks his arm.

"Yeah, nice going."

"What? How am I supposed to remember every one of your twisted lies?" he teases.

"My lies?" she says, incredulous.

"I'm kidding!" he laughs, leaning close to his door before

she can smack him. "Seriously, though, what do you make of Brett? That's super weird, right?"

"Super weird," Clara agrees.

"I mean...do you think Jo could be right? Could he be stealing from everyone?"

"I just..." Clara muses, "I just can't imagine that he would? Or that he'd get away with it all these years? I know for a fact there's no money missing from Jo's trust—"

"Do you, though? If he's been pulling money out for her monthly allowance and not giving her all of it—"

"Is that what she's said? I thought she was worried about the balances in her account."

"Well she is, but she's also said that her allowance amounts have changed—that they aren't consistent."

"Hmmm. Well, I guess I can't be 100% sure," she admits.

As Toby drives, he ponders potential next steps. They can't continue to stalk Brett. Eventually, he's going to notice an old Buick constantly on the road behind him. And it's not like they can gain access to his bank records. So what next?

"I think we have to confront him," Toby concludes.

"What?" Clara asks in shock. "That's a terrible idea. What is he going to say? 'Yes, I steal from my patients, you got me','" she says, imitating a man's voice. "He's just going to deny it, and we won't be able to tell if it's true or not."

"But think about it, Clara: what other options do we have? We can't prove anything."

"Maybe if we keep looking into it..." she trails off, realizing as the words leave her lips that it's a dead end. "We may just have to let it be," Clara says. "I know it's terrible to think that someone could be taking advantage of the elderly, but it's not really our place. And if we bring to light these accusations and we're incorrect..."

Toby sighs. "I just can't stand the thought of him getting

away with it. If Jo's right, she's basically been gas-lighted for the last couple of years."

"By me," Clara says, her voice low.

"It wasn't your fault—"

"I just assumed—she had all these other signs of early dementia…"

"It's okay, Clar," Toby says, attempting to comfort her as he pulls up in front of her house. "I'm glad you came today."

"Next time, a little warning would be nice," she says, smiling in spite of herself.

"I'll think about it," Toby teases.

Clara opens the car door and walks to her door.

"Hey, actually," Toby calls. "Come to Bunco with me Sunday!"

Clara turns, shaking her head. "Seriously?"

"It will be after your event, so you'll be all relaxed," Toby teases. "C'mon, it'll be fun, I promise. And Rowena makes these Russian—"

"Wedding cookies?" Clara cuts in excitedly.

"Yes! I had no idea what they were, but they're amazing."

"Okay, you should have mentioned the cookies earlier," she says, pointing a finger at him.

"See you then!" he says, sliding back into the seat and waving as he drives away.

CHAPTER 32

"Are you sure we should bother her?" Clara asks, twisting her hands nervously on the step.

"She might not want to go, but we should at least ask," Toby shrugs.

The door opens, and Jo stands behind the glass.

"Hey, Jo," Toby says, smiling. "Clara and I are going to Bunco and wanted to invite you to come with."

Jo frowns. "I don't want to see them," she says.

"Well it doesn't start for thirty minutes or so. Okay if we visit for a bit?" Toby asks.

She opens the door, motioning for them to come inside.

Toby walks to the couch and settles into his regular cushion. Jo sits next to him, turning down the volume on the TV.

"What is this?" Toby asks, peering at the screen.

"Sundays are terrible for TV," Jo explains.

"Clearly," Toby says, laughing. Only then does he notice Clara still standing. "Oh!" he says, launching off the sofa. "Take my seat," he says.

"No, it's okay—"

"Seriously," he says, moving out of the way. She takes him

up on it, settling in next to Jo. Toby picks up a chair from the kitchen and carries it to the living room.

"So how've you been feeling?" he asks Jo. "How's the bed?"

"I feel like I'm going to get lost in it," she laughs. "And my back isn't used to being so supported."

Toby grins. "That's a good problem, right?"

Clara's eyes are wide. Apparently he'd forgotten to tell her about his handy addition.

"Do you want to see Jo's bed, Clara?" Toby asks, his eyes twinkling.

"Ummm...absolutely," she says, standing up.

"Okay if I show her?" Toby asks, already in motion.

Jo waves them off, apparently engrossed in the terrible TV show.

"What did you do, Toby?" Clara whispers as he rushes through the kitchen.

Turning through the doorway, Clara sees Precious curled up on the bed. Deja vu, she thinks, grimacing slightly. Toby climbs onto the bed to pet the cat and, as he does, she sees it.

"Did you build this?" Clara asks in awe.

"I did."

"It's perfect," she says, running her fingers along the handrail. "I can't believe you got her to sleep in this thing."

"I didn't actually know if she'd like it, but when she was in the care facility, I had nothing better to do. Figured it was worth a shot."

"It's impressive, Tob," she says, and Toby grins. Surprisingly, Precious doesn't scurry off when Clara puts her hand out. She turns her smashed face toward her, wary, but tolerating her for the moment.

"She's never let me pet her before," Clara says, stroking the soft, white fur.

"It's because I'm here."

"Thanks for that," she laughs.

. . .

BACK IN THE LIVING ROOM, they find Jo still on the couch.

"So. TV is terrible," Toby repeats. "Seems like you'd want something else to do this evening."

Jo gives him a sidelong glance. "I'm not dressed."

"You look dressed to me," he says.

"Not well enough for that group."

"I could help you," Clara says.

"She could give you a makeover!" Toby says excitedly. "Make Roy stop in his tracks when he sees you."

"I don't care what Roy thinks," she responds, flustered. "And my face still hasn't gone back to normal."

"You honestly can't even tell," Toby insists. "And even if you don't like them, you may as well eat their cookies. We could bring up a whole bunch of controversial topics. It would be hilarious."

Jo looks between the two of them skeptically.

"Please?" Clara asks, putting her hands together.

"Fine," Jo sighs. "But if I look like a clown, I'm canceling."

"Okay, just hurry!" Toby says. "We've only got about twelve minutes."

Jo hoists herself upright and walks toward the bedroom with Clara in tow.

"I THINK...THIS one would be great," Clara says, pulling a floral blouse from the closet. "And it goes with those pants you like."

Jo nods. "I haven't worn that in ages."

"It's beautiful. Here, I'll go out so you can change."

Clara moves outside the door and waits. Though Jo did flash her a suspicious look at one point in the living room, she didn't say anything. I do look quite different when I'm dressed normally and not in my Simply Living uniform, she thinks. And I'm almost never wearing makeup when I work. Maybe the mascara makes enough of a difference? Jo was so worked up last time, I doubt she'd have any idea who was sitting on her couch. Unless it was Brett.

"Ready," Jo calls, and Clara reenters the room.

"It's perfect," Clara says. The soft pastels compliment Jo's skin tone flawlessly. "Can I curl your hair?" she asks.

"With a curling iron?" Jo responds, her eyes widening.

"Yes," Clara laughs. "I'll be careful, I promise."

"It's under the sink," Jo instructs and Clara moves to the bathroom, opening the cupboard. Finding it easily, she plugs it in and then turns to Jo.

"While this heats up, I can do your makeup if you want?" Clara suggests.

Jo nods, and Clara picks up a compact and eyeshadow palette.

"Any color okay?" she asks. "You won't look like a clown, I promise."

Jo raises her eyebrows, but gives her the go ahead. Clara clicks open the box and gently presses the foam brush into a shimmering neutral powder.

"Close your eyes," she says softly. As she applies the shadow, she says, "What was your wedding like?"

"It was nothing like the big weddings nowadays," Jo answers, attempting to keep her face still.

"How so?"

"Well, for one thing, we didn't plan it years in advance. When we were ready to get married, the whole community kind of pulled together and got us what we needed."

"Really?"

"I was in a small town, it might have been different in the city."

"What was your dress like?"

Jo sighs, "It was beautiful. My mother made it for me. I have a picture over there," she says, pointing toward the nightstand. Clara rises and takes a few steps to see it up close. Though the picture is blurry, she can clearly see the lace detailing, the beautiful A-line, and the three-quarter-length sleeves.

"I didn't ever learn to sew," Clara says.

"I learned the basics," Jo says, taking the small mirror from Clara's hands and inspecting her face. "But I couldn't make a dress."

"Do you like it?" Clara asks, and Jo nods.

"Marriage was different then, too," Jo remembers. "We didn't ever expect it to be something it wasn't."

Clara sits next to her on the bed. "How long were you married?"

"Forty-six years."

"Wow," Clara breathes. "You're going to give me your tips right?" she says jokingly.

"It doesn't work that way," Jo chuckles, motioning at her hair.

"Oh," Clara says, "you're right. I'm sure the iron is plenty hot by now."

"How were the bubbles?" Jo asks, and Clara stops mid-stride.

"Bubbles?" she asks, her eyebrows furrowing.

"Yesterday. The bubbles," she repeats.

A broad smile spreads across Clara's face. "The employee appreciation event," she says, impressed. "I can't believe you remembered that. They were a huge hit."

TOBY IS SURPRISINGLY INVESTED in the family court case on TV. He watches with disgust as the plaintiff attempts to throw his spouse under the bus. Precious is settled on his lap, nudging his hand whenever he forgets to pet her. When Jo and Clara reenter the living room, he looks up and a grin spreads across his face.

"You look amazing!" he says, shifting Precious to the next cushion and standing. "So beautiful, Jo."

"I'm only doing this for the cookies," Jo says. Toby laughs and quickly opens the door, allowing Clara and Jo to exit, then picks up the wheelchair and sets it up on the walkway. After shutting the door, he moves next to Jo and helps her navigate the steps.

They don't even have to knock once they cross the street, Rowena is already waiting for them at the door.

"Jo!" she exclaims, taking in her outfit. "You look lovely, dear. We're all so glad you came. We've been so worried about you," Rowena gushes. Jo waves her off, pressing against the armrests to stand up. Clara folds up the chair as Toby supports Jo to the entrance.

Rowena moves to allow them in and instructs Clara to place the chair behind the door.

"We have an odd number today," Rowena announces, "but that's no problem. Roy, can you bring over an extra chair from the kitchen?" Roy doesn't answer. He stands frozen, staring at Jo.

"You okay there Roy?" Toby asks, amusement in his tone.

Roy clears his throat. "I can get a chair," he says finally, walking into the kitchen. Toby nudges Jo, laughing under his breath.

"Oh stop," Jo whispers. "It's just shocking to see me without my hair sticking up."

"I don't think that's it," Clara says. "You look amazing, Jo."

"Take a seat," Rowena instructs as she follows Roy into the kitchen. Moments later, she rolls her cart into the room and begins to distribute her confections.

"You weren't kidding," Clara says in amazement. "Look at those."

"Worth it, right?" Toby teases.

After filling up their plates and reminding Clara of the rules, the game begins. As promised, Toby starts the conversation.

"Do you know what I heard on the news the other day?" he starts, and Clara holds her breath preemptively. "They said that they're starting to give out student loans that people aren't even going to have to repay."

Roy turns to him. "What do you mean they won't have to repay?"

"I mean the government is just going to pay for their schooling for them, like free tuition."

Roy pushes back from the table. "Jo, have you ever heard of something so crazy?" he says turning to her. "Back in my day, we had to work for every step up in society. They weren't just handing out free University," he scoffs.

Clara covers her mouth, pretending to cough.

"I hear you, Roy. It's ridiculous," Jo says, winking at Toby as she takes a bite of her cookie.

So far, so good, Toby thinks, tallying a few more topics just in case the women get bored and begin tittering about all of their friend's progeny.

"This sweet tea is delicious, Rowena," Clara says, and Rowena thanks her. Toby watches the interaction around him and grins. Then he rolls the dice.

CHAPTER 33

"Look at us, overlapping shifts more than twice in a month," Abby says as she passes Toby at the bar.

"I know, right? I think Clint must have realized that having his best servers on at the same time is a smart move."

"The day that Clint makes a smart move…" Abby says under her breath, winking at Toby as she whisks two margaritas from the counter and turns back to the dining room.

"Hey," Toby calls after her. "What are you doing after this?"

"Probably walking slowly home, trying to be late enough that I won't get roped into watching a classic movie with my parents," she says grinning.

"Well...I think I could help with that."

"Yeah?" she asks, pausing in the hall.

"Want to go to Cinemagic? They have a french indie film I want to see."

"French indie?" she asks, her eyes widening slightly in

surprise. "I didn't peg you as a guy who would be into that," she teases. "But sure, I'm in."

"Cool," he says. "I'll get tickets."

Abby smiles, turning on her heel and heading toward her table.

AT THE END of their shifts—after cashing out tips—Abby walks toward Toby near the hostess stand. Toby waits, breathing deeply and trying to remain calm. With sweaty palms and a racing heart, he opens the door for her and turns to walk up the hill.

"My car is back at the house, but it's only a short walk. You sure your parents won't mind?"

"I texted my dad, it's all good," she says, tucking her hands in her coat pockets. "I've never been to Cinemagic before, but I've heard it's a fun theater."

"Yeah, I really like it. It's one of the oldest theaters on the west coast—single screen."

"No way?"

Toby nods. "I don't know why I get a kick out of stuff like that."

"It's like a reminder of a past era."

"It just feels slower, more deliberate, if that makes sense?"

"I get it," Abby says, slightly out of breath.

Toby approaches the Buick and unlocks it.

"This is your car?"

"Technically I'm just using it. It's my neighbor's, but she doesn't drive anymore."

"Your neighbor?"

"Yeah, she's eighty-seven."

"No way! And she lets you use her car? It's pretty sweet."

Toby laughs, dropping into his seat as Abby does the same.

"Well I'm impressed," she says. "And also slightly nervous that I'm going to spill something and ruin the seat."

"I'm definitely not letting you eat in here," Toby teases. He turns the car around and sets off in the direction of the theater, coming to a full stop at every stop sign and not running any yellow lights. He laughs internally at his obvious desire to impress Abby, but who knows if she's looking for a rule follower? Maybe she wants a risk-taker—someone who shakes his fist at society and...stop signs. Already feeling the stress of living up to unknown expectations, he takes a deep breath. I can't pretend to be anything I'm not, Toby reasons. Either she'll like me or she won't. End of story.

"So tell me about your family? You've heard about mine," Abby says, reaching into her purse for chapstick and applying it generously. Toby catches himself staring instead of answering the question.

"My family is...a little crazier than yours," he starts. "My sister Clara lives here in Portland—that's actually why I moved out here. My dad and his wife live in Minnesota where I'm originally from—"

"Which part? I have a good friend from Minnesota."

"Twin Cities area. I'm a student at Madison."

"You're currently a student?" she asks skeptically.

"Was. Am? I deferred a year, so technically I'm still enrolled, just not taking classes at the moment."

"Why did you defer?" she asks sincerely.

"I thought this was about my family?" Toby hedges.

"Well...now I want to know this."

"Fair," Toby sighs. "My mom actually passed away when I was young and I don't really see eye to eye with my dad. I did three years at Madison and realized that I was headed into a career I wasn't passionate about—"

"What career?"

"Engineering," Toby states, slowing to parallel park on the street near the theater.

"Math," Abby complains, lifting her hand into a thumbs down.

Toby laughs, "Hey, I actually like the math, it's just...I couldn't see myself sitting in a cubicle working equations all day, you know?"

"Hey, the math part doesn't even appeal to me, so I get it," Abby says, picking up her purse and opening her door now that the car is motionless. They step out to the sidewalk and Toby points to the theater just up the road.

"I'm sorry about your mom," Abby says softly as they begin walking.

"Me too. I miss her every day. We lived with her here for a few years when I was young, then moved back with my dad when she passed. Every once in a while I pass something that reminds me of something we did together. But my memories are pretty spotty from that time. When she got sick...I think I blocked it all out."

"I don't blame you," Abby empathizes. She reaches out and pulls his hand into hers. Surprisingly, it feels natural, despite Toby's lack of relationship experience. He can't help but grin as they walk the remaining block to the theater.

THE NEXT MORNING, bright and early, Toby is on Jo's doorstep. He knocks and waits patiently for her to open the door. He can hear the TV on, though that's not necessarily an indicator that Jo is watching it. Even though she sleeps in her bed these days, Toby has noticed that she still keeps the TV on. Comfort, maybe? Or just an old habit? Regardless, the sound makes it difficult for her to hear when she's not in the living room.

A thought occurs to him, and he begins to knock out a

rhythm, hoping that Jo will hear it and remember their very first meeting. He can't keep the smile off his face until the door opens. Jo stands in the entry looking disheveled, her eyes slightly vacant. Toby's stomach drops.

"Hey Jo," he says gently. "I wanted to check in on you and see how you're doing."

"Are you selling something?" she asks, her voice harsh. Her white hair stands on end and there are dark circles under her eyes.

"Nope, definitely not," he answers.

"We have a 'No Soliciting' sign for the neighborhood," Jo reminds him.

"I'm actually your neighbor, I live right over there," he points to the house next door.

"Well I've never seen you before."

Toby, though her comment pierces him more deeply than he'd like to admit, slaps a smile on his face. "That's because I just moved in," he says cheerily. "I'm trying to meet all the neighbors."

"I'm sorry," she says, "I didn't mean to be rude. Salesmen are doing whatever they can these days to get through the door."

"Oh I know, it's smart to be cautious," he agrees.

"There's supposed to be a storm this weekend," she says, worriedly inspecting the clouds overhead.

"So I've heard," Toby replies. "Are you ready for it?"

"Mostly. I have groceries and a few books. I'm worried about one spot on my roof."

"Well let's have a look at it. That's what neighbors do, right?"

Jo nods and opens the door for him. Toby follows her to the kitchen, despite the fact that when he checked his weather app this morning, it showed nothing but scattered clouds for the next three days.

CHAPTER 34

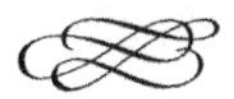

"She didn't remember a thing," Toby explains, leaning back in the beanbag chair and putting his phone on speaker.

"Seriously?" Clara asks, her voice concerned.

"Yeah, I helped her with her roof. She was convinced it was going to storm today."

"Wow. I wonder what happened? That's so odd that from one day to the next…"

"I know."

"Did she mention anything about Brett?" Clara questions.

"Nope. I actually said something about Simply Living and she just stared at me. It was like she was a different person," Toby explains. "A different person that's mostly the same...but different." He sighs. "I know I'm not making any sense."

"No, I've definitely seen it before with some of the patients I've worked with. It's scary, Tob. I'm sorry you had to see that. Patients in that state can get violent. Sounds like you dealt with it really well."

Stretching out he closes his eyes, thinking.

"So what now?" Clara asks.

"I don't know," Toby admits. "I hate the idea of starting all over again with her, but I'll totally do it. And as for Brett…" he sits up, an idea forming in his mind. "Hey, Clar? Do you by chance have access to employee files at work? You're a team leader, right?"

"Right," Clara admits hesitantly. "But I only have access to the employees on my team."

"Are you sure? Have you ever tried to access anyone else's?"

"Well, no, but—"

"Could you just try? If it doesn't work, that's totally fine, but it's the only thing I can think of."

"What exactly would I be looking for?" She asks, less than thrilled at the idea of snooping into Brett's personal files.

"Well, I was just thinking—if he's been doing this for a while, there have to be some complaints on his file, right? I'm sure they've recorded Jo's complaints—regardless of whether they think they're valid or not, they should be there right?"

"They should, but Tob—if those complaints are all from dementia patients...Doesn't really hold much weight."

"But he's not the only one seeing these patients. If he has all these complaints and nobody else does—"

"It's true, if there was a pattern that cut and dry, it would at least give us something to go off," she agrees.

"Thanks, Clar."

"Hey, I didn't say I'd do it."

Toby smiles. "Thanks, Clar."

On another rare lunch shift, Toby is disappointed to see that Abby isn't working today. Though he still doesn't know her well, something about her has caught his interest, as much as he hates to admit it. Not that he is opposed to meeting someone...it just doesn't seem like the best timing.

The lunch rush is surprisingly intense with a constant buzz of people lining up at the hostess station. Though, Toby realizes, he doesn't have much to compare it to. Maybe it's typically this busy.

Regardless, by the time 2:30pm rolls around, he's beat. He cashes out his tips and rolls up his apron, excited to go home and take a nap. Thankfully, he works the late dinner shift tonight, not arriving until 7pm. Again, he feels a letdown that Abby won't be there. He groans, amazed that his emotions are already being upended by a girl he's spent time with twice, and who probably hasn't thought twice about him today.

Setting his apron on a shelf behind the bar, he quickly uses the bathroom and returns to the hallway. Pulling out his phone, he is surprised to see two notifications from Clara. Retrieving his apron and leaning against the wall, he pulls up the messages.

>Hey Tob. Just FYI...I broke it off with Ian. Thought you'd want to know XOXO

>PS Don't you dare say I told you so.

What? Toby's heart constricts thinking of his sister. Searching desperately for words, he types and retypes a message.

>What? How did this happen? I hope

DELETE

>Clara dang. So sorry. Let's

DELETE
>Back on the scene! Want to
DELETE

Ugh. I'm such an idiot, he thinks, frustrated at his inability to compose an appropriate response. A thought occurs to him and he rushes back to the kitchen.

"Hey, I didn't use my lunch today," Toby says. "Can I put in an order to go?"

"Do whatever you want, man," one of the cooks says, annoyed at being interrupted.

Toby rushes to the computer and puts an order in for chicken marsala. Clara seemed to enjoy that last time she came.

>Are you at work or home right now?

He sends the message, then stares at the screen for confirmation that she saw it. Three dots appear and he holds his breath.

>Work. Headed over to the SL office in 20 to work on admin stuff

Perfect. Though it takes longer than he'd hoped, his order eventually makes an appearance, and Toby rushes up the hill. Not even bothering to change, he jumps in the driver's seat of the Buick, only then realizing that his car keys are on his kitchen counter. Setting the paper bag on the passenger side, he runs inside to grab them. At least that gives him the chance to throw off his bow tie.

Sliding back into his seat, he hurriedly straps a seatbelt across the food so it won't slip to the floor while he drives. He forces himself to keep the speed limit and drive responsibly the entire way to Simply Living. See, I do this even without a girl sitting next to me, he thinks. And next week I have to get this thing registered.

Out of habit, he parks two blocks away. Though he realizes as soon as he pulls the keys out of the ignition that there's no need for secrecy this time, getting the Buick between two SUV's took too much time for him to be willing to move it. Picking up the bag and double checking that he put the keys in his pocket, he walks toward the building.

His heart beats a little faster as he opens the doors. I'm not doing anything wrong...today, he thinks, smirking in spite of himself. Forcing his face to look professional as he approaches the desk, he waves at a stout woman currently talking on the phone.

"I know, that's what they told me," she says, her southern drawl smooth like honey. Toby doesn't even mind that he has to wait. He could listen to this all day.

"Oh honey, I'm so sorry. It seems like they would have to figure that out for y'all....mhmmm.....I know. Well, baby, I've got someone here at the desk, but I'll call you back tonight. Love you baby."

She places the phone back on the receiver and turns to Toby. "Hey there, so sorry about that! My daughter is going through some things, you know how it is."

Toby smiles as if he does in fact know how it is. "I'm looking for Clara, do you know which office I could find her in?"

"Absolutely, she just walked in about ten minutes before you. If you walk down the hall, then take your first right, you'll see her in the third office on your left," she says, standing and leaning over the counter to point the way.

"Thanks. Hope your daughter finds a solution," he says, waving as he starts down the hall.

"Thanks sweetheart!" she calls after him.

He's still smiling when he gets to Clara's office and remembers the reason for his trip. His expression immediately sobers as he walks through the door.

Clara's eyes are more puffy than usual, though anyone else would probably assume she simply had a bad night of sleep. "Hey," she sighs, setting down her pen. Tears immediately well up in her eyes. Toby sets the bag on the desk and pulls her up out of her seat into a bear hug.

"Clar, I'm so sorry," he whispers. Her shoulders shake and he holds her, not saying anything else. What does a twenty-one year old kid with virtually zero relationship experience say in a situation like this? He is utterly useless.

She pulls back and moves again behind the desk to grab her tissues.

"Ugh, sorry. I didn't mean to break down like this," she apologizes, blowing her nose.

"No, are you kidding? Break down all you want."

She laughs. "I really do feel at peace about the situation, but it's still just...hard to say goodbye to a long relationship like that."

Toby nods.

"Honestly, I knew all along that Ian wasn't exactly what I was looking for, but he has some really amazing qualities that made me justify it," she explains, throwing her hands in the air and slumping back into her rolling chair. Swiveling to face Toby as he sits across from her, she continues, "Like I felt so secure with him. He always had an answer and had his life all planned out. It was safe."

"I get that," he says gently. "And it's not that I hated him—"

"No, I get it. It's true. He is serious all the time, and I didn't love that he only pulled the serious side out of me! I got to thinking about having a family and what that would look like...All I could see was Ian teaching our kids about 401k's and—and refusing to let them dump out their Lego collection."

Toby laughs and is grateful when Clara joins him. "Well, as I have literally no advice to give, I brought you some comfort food," he says, pulling out the container. "I realized just now that Ian was with you when you originally got this at Bob's, so I'm really sorry if this is a trigger," he says seriously, but Clara waves him off.

"No, this is awesome. With everything going on, I only brought a cheese stick and granola bar for lunch." She reaches for the cutlery packet and immediately pops the top open and digs in.

"Did you bring anything for yourself?" she asks, her mouth full of chicken and noodles.

"No, I eat there almost daily. Starts to lose its appeal. Plus, I had a late breakfast."

"Cereal?" she teases.

"No," he answers, feigning offense, "I actually cooked myself a breakfast sandwich today."

Clara's eyes widen in surprise, and he continues, "It doesn't matter that it was microwaved out of the freezer."

She grins, rolling her eyes. "Well at least it's something."

"It was gross. I'm just going to say it."

Clara snorts. "Don't do that! A noodle is going to come out of my nose!"

"I'll go get you some water," he offers and steps into the hall. Walking back toward the lobby, he finds the water dispenser near the back window. He picks up a cup, fills it, and turns, almost running into someone.

"So sorry," he says, looking down to make sure no water spilled on his white shirt.

"In a hurry?" the man says, and Toby looks up in surprise. Seeing Brett's face, he can almost feel the blood draining from his own face. Brett moves to the coffee maker and puts in a new filter. Hoping to escape before he is recognized, he moves toward the hallway.

"Hey," Brett calls, making the connection. "You're that guy I saw at the roller skating rink. You were with Jo, right?"

"Oh yeah, I forgot about that," he answers, turning slightly to acknowledge him, but continuing on. He hears footsteps behind him.

"What were you thinking?" Brett accuses.

Toby turns to face him with a questioning look.

"That was incredibly dangerous. Why in the world would you put someone like Jo on roller-skates?"

"I was just trying to get her out and about," Toby answers honestly, again trying to cut the conversation short, but Brett puts out a hand.

"You've been spending a lot of time with her, then, huh?"

"I guess so, she's my neighbor and she's pretty lonely," Toby stammers, starting to sweat.

"So what's your angle? Hoping she'll die soon and leave you money?"

Toby's face pinches into a look of disgust. "No, actually, she's—"

"Hey, what's going on?" Clara calls from a few doors down and Toby spins toward her. "Brett?"

"Hey Clara, how's it going?"

Clara walks toward them, her slight heels clicking on the wooden floor. "So I see you've met my brother."

Brett points his thumb toward him. “This guy? He’s your brother?”

Clara nods, standing with her arms across her chest.

“Are you okay?” Brett asks, noticing her red-rimmed eyes.

“Fine,” she answers bluntly. “What are you two talking about?”

“Did you know that your bro took one of our patients out roller-skating? Could’ve killed her.”

Clara shifts her weight. “We talked about it,” she admits, glancing at Toby, “but it sounds like they had a great time.”

“That woman is crazy, Clara. She’s rude and accuses everyone of—”

“Not everyone,” Clara cuts him off.

Brett leans back as if she smacked him. “That’s your statement? You think I’m the problem here?”

Clara sighs, “I don’t know, Brett, but it does seem odd that multiple clients have accused you of stealing from them.”

“It’s because I deal with all the dementia patients! Of course I’m going to be accused more. They’re looking to blame anyone, and I just happen to be there,” he fumes.

“Whoa,” Clara says, putting her hands out. “I get it—”

“Then why were you burying a box in the park?” Toby blurts out. Clara and Brett both turn to look at him with wide eyes.

“What are you talking about?” Brett asks, his voice low.

“I was walking on the path at the Green and I saw you. When I walked toward you to say hi, I stopped because you started digging a hole by the stream,” he lies, shoving his hands in his pocket.

“You’ve been spying on me?” Brett concludes, his voice menacing.

“No, like I said—” Toby starts, but Clara cuts him off.

“What were you doing burying a box in the park?” she asks, putting her hands on her hips.

"Who cares?" he spits. "What a guy does in his free time is his own business."

"Not if it involves stealing from the elderly!" Toby shoots back.

"You seriously—?" Brett's face turns red and his hands ball into fists. He stomps past them down the hall.

"If it's not a big deal, why won't you tell us?" Toby calls before he gets far.

Brett spins on his heels. "I was burying a hamster, okay?" he shouts, then looks around as his voice echoes off the walls. The southern woman leans over the counter and shoots him a dirty look.

He moves closer. "I was burying my daughter's hamster. Our backyard is all paved and landscaped, so I figured a park was the next best place," he explains, anger still lacing his tone.

Toby stares in shock. "Is that even allowed?" he asks under his breath.

"No idea! But I had to get that thing out of our freezer."

Clara recoils in disgust.

"You happy?" Brett asks, throwing his hands out to the side. "Disgusting, yes. But I'm not stealing from old people." He turns and stomps down the hallway, forgetting about his coffee, and slams the door to his office.

TOBY TURNS to Clara and motions for her to follow him back to her office, water cup in hand. Upon shutting the door, they both burst into gut-wrenching laughter.

CHAPTER 35

After sleeping in, Toby showers and meanders to Jo's to check in. It's only been a day since he's seen her, but that last interaction was disturbing to say the least. Standing at the door, he knocks. The TV is silent today. Odd, but maybe she finally slept in, too?

He knocks again, but doesn't hear anything. Suddenly, the blinds erupt into motion inside the bay window and Toby jumps back, catching himself with the metal railing. Precious is frantically mewing in the window, staring at him with desperate eyes. Adrenaline kicks in as Toby recognizes that something is terribly wrong.

Searching for a way in, Toby remembers that the window near the kitchen is loose. When they were out back looking at the Buick, he had noticed it and meant to fix it for her. Procrastination for the win. Barreling around the side of the house, he pulls a trash can from the neighbors and sets it under the window. When standing on it, the window hits him waist-high and it's simple to jimmy it open and crawl inside. As soon as his shoes hit the linoleum, Precious comes running, pawing at her food bowl.

"Sorry girl, I'll be right back," he says, dusting himself off and scanning the room. Poking his head into the living room and finding it empty, he runs toward the bedroom. As he opens the door, he hears her.

"Help," she croaks, her voice hoarse.

"Jo?" he calls, and not finding her in the bed, turns to the bathroom. Jo lies on the floor completely naked, one leg bent at an unnatural angle, propped up on the tub. Her face is smeared with dried blood and her nose is swollen to the point that he almost doesn't recognize her.

"Jo," he breathes, grabbing the towel that lays next to her and covering her body. She is shivering and he curses under his breath. "Jo, I'm not going to move you because I don't know what's broken, but I'm going to get help."

"Precious," she says softly, then closes her eyes and lays her cheek on the cold linoleum.

"I've got it, I'll take care of her," he says, his eyes filling with tears. Pulling out his cell, he begins to dial and then remembers why he used the handheld last time. This call needs to be traceable. Running to the kitchen, he picks up the receiver and again dials the dreaded number, Precious pawing him as he waits for someone to pick up.

CHAPTER 36

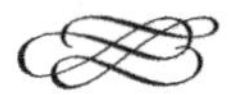

Clara enters the ER waiting area alone this time, scanning for her brother and finding him in the same back corner. Tears spring to her eyes as she winds her way through the empty chairs. Toby sits with slumped shoulders and his head in his hands, his curls making a curtain around his face.

"How bad is it?" she asks softly, placing a hand on his back. He lifts his head and looks at her with red-rimmed eyes. A tear slips down his cheek and his lips tremble.

"Oh Tob," Clara says, wrapping his arms around him. Tears escape from the corner of her eyes as she squeezes him tightly, attempting to ward away the hurt. Not having any wise words come to mind, she holds him in silence, staring at the textured hospital wall.

After a few long minutes, Toby finally pulls away and wipes his eyes as he takes a deep breath, exhaling loudly.

"She was so cold, Clara. I have no idea how long she had been stuck like that. Alone, afraid, in what I can only assume was a massive amount of pain—"

"I know, it's awful," Clara agrees. "At least you found her before—"

Toby closes his eyes and Clara stops short. "I'm not sure I did," he says weakly. "They wouldn't let me ride with her this time. It's bad."

"But you got there. Even if she doesn't make it...she won't be in pain."

Toby takes another cleansing breath and slides back in the seat, stretching his long legs across the tiled floor.

"Toby, I don't think you understand what a blessing you've been in her life. I know I told you about when I first tried to make contact, but I don't think I told you everything."

Toby turns to her, his eyes intent.

Clara sighs. "I was embarrassed that I had failed so miserably." She holds the edges of her coat and pulls them tight, wrapping her arms around herself protectively. "I had such high hopes, and then...the rejection was so painful. I had all these ideas about how I would learn so much more about Mom talking to Jo. How I would finally have the endless questions in my mind answered, or even just hear that she—" Clara purses her lips, trying to contain her emotions, "—that she talked about us, you know?"

Toby nods, listening with rapt attention.

"I showed up at her door that day and introduced myself and she immediately shut me out. She said that I was money-grubbing, just trying to get into her will. I don't even think she knew I was actually related to her, she just slammed the door and didn't even give me the chance...And here I had literally moved across the country to get to know her," she shakes her head in frustration.

"Is that the only reason you came out here?" Toby asks, surprised. "I thought the thing with Nike—"

"Well of course I didn't just come here *just* for that, but that's the reason I chose the Nike internship over the other options. I had other offers—one in DC, one in Toronto," she says, listing them off.

"Did you try again?" Toby asks.

"Of course I did," she says, her eyes flashing. "I tried at least three more times—I went at different times of day and kept telling myself that I was just catching her at a bad moment. Sometimes she remembered me and that made it even worse, and when she didn't...it was somehow more hurtful to go through it all again."

"And that's why you took the job at Simply Living?"

Clara nods. "Yeah, she said something about it on one of those wonderful visits. I looked into it and, since I needed a part-time job anyway, I figured that would at least give me a legitimate reason to continue to go over. You know the rest."

Toby slings an arm around her, and her head drops to rest on his shoulder.

"Then you showed up, and she immediately took to you. I'm sorry I didn't respond well, but—"

"No, I get it. That must have been really hurtful."

"Yeah," she agrees. "I just don't know what I did wrong."

"Well, if it helps, you kind of paved the way. Because you had mentioned at some point that she didn't respond well to someone showing up and announcing their family connection, I avoided saying anything like that."

"I guess that's true," she laughs, still sniffing and wiping her nose with a tissue she had in her purse. "I still can't believe you sold the car and rented a house right next to her."

Toby shakes with laughter, recognizing the ridiculousness of it now. "At the time, it seemed like a brilliant idea."

"Well I think it was—just slightly risky. And possibly a bit crazy."

"I can't help it. I know the way I do things seems nuts to you and Dad, but it just feels right, you know? And when something doesn't feel right...it's really hard for me to continue on. It feels like a constant, crushing weight. I know you probably think that makes me weak and selfish—"

"Those are Dad's words, Toby. I'll admit, I've had those thoughts and I know I've agreed with that assessment at times, but seeing how your process has done so much good—well, I may not understand it, but I think I can appreciate it now."

Toby squeezes her shoulder, and she lifts her head to meet his eyes.

"I think I've gone most of my life with such a linear view of things. But this whole thing with Ian...I get it. I get how you can feel trapped even when something seems to make sense."

Toby smiles, then whips his head toward the nurse's station as the door opens. A doctor in green scrubs walks through the door and scans the waiting room as Toby watches him hopefully. The doctor says something to one of the nurses and she points toward Toby and Clara. Breathing deeply, Toby stands and Clara holds his hand as they walk toward the doctor.

"Are you here for Jo?" he asks, his face sober.

They nod in unison.

"I don't have the best news, but it's also not the worst," he says, ushering them to sit in the chairs next to the doors. "Jo's body has suffered tremendously, but you found her just in time. We were able to stabilize her."

"Is she in any pain?" Toby asks.

"No, she's sleeping. We've got her hooked up to an IV with pain meds to keep her comfortable."

"Will she recover?" Clara questions hopefully.

The doctor takes a breath before answering. "This stroke was much larger than the first. Even with the blood thinners she was on, she sustained a lot of damage...especially after being alone for so long," he explains. "Her hip is badly broken, and normally we would consider fixing it, but she'll be bedridden regardless. Even with good care," he sighs apologetically, "I don't think she'll last more than a few weeks."

Toby nods, but his eyes seem to glaze over.

"Do you know if there's any family we should—"

"We are family," Toby jumps in. "We're her grandchildren."

"Oh!" the doctor answers, surprised. "I was under the impression that you were her neighbor."

"I'm that, too," Toby says.

"Well if you can present your ID at the nurse's station, they can take you back. You may want to go home and get some rest, though. I doubt she'll be lucid for at least another twelve hours."

They thank the doctor, then take the few steps to the desk to sign in.

"Do you have a shift you need to get to?" Clara asks while they wait for their wristbands.

"I called and let them know that I wouldn't be working for a few days."

"They were okay with that?"

"Yeah, I told them the situation. What about you?"

"I think I'll probably head home and come back tomorrow, if that's okay?"

"Sounds good. I can keep her company for now. I'll go home and feed Precious tonight and sleep at home, then head back in the morning."

"I'll be here first thing," she assures him. After putting on their bands, Toby gives Clara a small wave as he heads down the hall.

CHAPTER 37

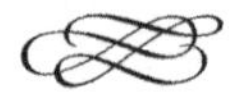

"Hey, Jo," Toby says gently, watching her eyelids flutter open for the first time all day.

"You've been getting some great beauty sleep," he says, attempting to draw her attention and help her focus. Her eyes float around the room aimlessly at first, but then stop on his face.

"Precious is fed and happy," he says, preempting her eventual question.

"Wh—wh—?" she stammers, her voice barely audible.

"We're in the hospital," he explains. "You fell, and I came over to see you—"

"You came?" she slurs, her eyes roving around the room wildly. Toby puts a hand on hers.

"I did, and Precious came to the window and alerted me—"

Jo focuses on him sharply.

"Yep, she saved you, Jo," he says tenderly and Jo relaxes slightly. "Are you comfortable?"

She grunts, and Toby laughs. There she is.

"Can I get you anything?" he asks, blinking to clear his misty eyes.

She motions to her throat, and Toby understands immediately.

"I'll get you some water."

WHEN HE RETURNS to Jo's room a few minutes later—a large plastic cup of ice water in his hand—she is sound asleep. He props her head up in a more natural position and leaves the water on her bedside table.

CHAPTER 38

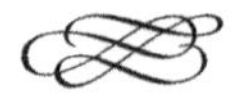

"I don't want to be here," Jo struggles with the words, lifting a spoonful of lime jello to her lips.

"Are you sure? They do have good snacks," Toby teases. Clara sits next to him on the slightly oversized chair.

Jo rolls her eyes. "Precious," she says.

"I'm sure she misses you, too. But I think we need to seriously talk about this, Jo. The doctor—" Clara starts, but Jo cuts her off.

"Doctor's. Poisoning me," Jo whispers, her voice crackly and her eyes wide.

"Jo, there's no way—" Clara begins, but Toby puts a hand on her arm.

"That's exactly why Clara wants to talk with you about this, Jo," Toby whispers, leaning in conspiratorially. "We have to get you out of here, but we can't let you go home alone. If there's poison in your system, you won't know it for weeks."

Clara turns to Toby with a horrified expression. He winks and continues, "Jo, how would you feel about staying with us for a few weeks? So that we can track your levels and make sure you're safe before taking you home?"

Jo looks between Clara and Toby, weighing her options. "Precious?" she asks finally.

"Absolutely," Toby answers and Clara pinches his thigh. He clenches his teeth and somehow maintains a mask of calm.

"Toby, can I have a word?" Clara asks, clearing her throat.

"Just one moment, Jo," Toby says calmly as Clara pulls him out the door and into the hall.

"Seriously?" she hisses. "What the—? I can't have a cat in my house!"

"Clara, there's no way it will cause a problem, it's for a few weeks at most—"

"Toby, when I agreed to this, I wasn't thinking that you'd be perpetuating a conspiracy theory—what were you thinking, by the way—or that I'd have to scoop a litter box—"

"Clara!" Toby says intently, holding her shoulders. "Breathe!"

She obediently closes her eyes and takes a few deep breaths.

"Okay, just hear me out," he pleads, holding up a hand when she tries to speak. "Two minutes, and then you can say whatever you want."

Clara takes another deep breath, leans against the wall, and nods.

"Alright," he lowers his voice. "Jo's dementia has been getting exponentially worse. There is no way that we can get her what she needs by reasoning with her. We have to jump in," he explains, gesticulating with his hands. "It doesn't matter if she 'knows' reality, she isn't living in reality! If we keep trying to argue with her or force her to see things the way we do, she'll just start seeing us as the enemy. It's not hurting her, and I promise that I would never agree to anything that would. If the end result is her being away from this place and feeling like she has allies, then that's best-case scenario, right? And as far as Precious is concerned, I'll do all the litter. I'll take care of all of it. We're going to have full-on medical equipment in there, so that's the least of my concerns."

As she begins to protest, Toby continues, "I'll have your carpets cleaned!"

"You don't have money to have my carpets cleaned, Toby!"

"I'll be getting my damage deposit back on the townhouse, that should cover it," he says, shoving his hands in his back pockets and stepping away.

Clara relaxes her shoulders. "Fine," she agrees, throwing up her hands. "But I swear, if I become a bad guy in this narrative you are creating—"

"Never, I promise. I'll find a way to work in all of your noble qualities," he assures her, flashing a cheesy grin. Clara rolls her eyes and stalks back into the room.

CHAPTER 39

Toby pulls his hair into a bun. With his final load of boxes in the Buick, his last tasks are sweeping and then wiping down the fridge. He mentally pats himself on the back for owning so little—moving his entire house only took three trips. Especially since he put his small table and chairs on the curb. They disappeared within the hour. Putting in his headphones, he turns on his energy playlist and gets to work.

After sweeping out each room thoroughly, he moves his pile down the hallway and into the living room. Out of the corner of his eye, he notices movement and jumps, pulling out his headphones.

"Hey, sorry to bust in on you," Abby says hesitantly, shifting her weight. "I did try to knock, but the door was open…"

"No, it's fine," Toby says, setting his phone on the counter and leaning the broom against the wall.

"I realized that I didn't have your phone number, and since you haven't been at work—I assumed this was your place since your car is parked out front—in the same place as when we went to the theater."

"That would have been awkward if you guessed wrong," he teases, dusting off his shirt.

"Yeah," she laughs, and her nose wrinkles. "So," she says, glancing around the room, "You're moving?"

"I am. Sorry I didn't say anything. I didn't have a chance—"

"No, it's not a big deal."

"Did Clint say anything? About why I haven't been at work?"

Abby shakes her head.

"I told you about my Grandma Jo, right?" Toby says, and she nods. "I'm sorry," he pauses, "I wish I had a place for us to sit. Want to go out on the step?"

"Sure," she says, smiling easily and moving outside.

Once they are settled on the concrete, Toby takes a deep breath and continues. "The other day, I went to check in on her and I could tell something wasn't right. Her cat was all pawing at the blinds and she didn't come to the door, so I went through a window and found her almost passed out on the floor. She had fallen, and—" he stops short, the image still too fresh in his mind.

"Wow, that must have been terrifying," Abby responds, eyes wide.

"Yeah, not cool. I called 9-1-1 and she's been in the hospital for the last week. It turns out she fell because she had another stroke. She's—she's not going to make it much longer and she doesn't want to be in the hospital."

"I don't blame her, hospitals are the worst," Abby whispers, pulling her knees close.

"I know. But, if she's not in the hospital, she has to be cared for night and day. It's not like she can just come home.

She has to have a catheter because she can't walk, pain meds..." he sighs. "The whole deal."

"That's a lot."

Toby nods. "She doesn't have anybody else."

"So you're moving in with her?" Abby asks.

"No, we're both going to move in with my sister Clara. Her house has a better set up, besides having to get everything up the stairs initially, and we figured it would be best if we could split the work. We'll have a lot of support from the staff at Simply Living—that's where my sister works; they do hospice care—and I'll do most of it during the day since she'll be working and finishing up a few classes."

"Are you done at Bob's?"

"No, but I'm only going to be working a few shifts a week until—" he catches his breath and Abby puts her hand on his arm.

"Thankfully, we can be paid through Simply Living to care for her. So even with working less shifts, I'll still be able to pay my part at Clara's," he explains. "Jo may not have registered her car, but she has great insurance," he laughs half-heartedly.

"That's really amazing, Toby. Seriously," she says soberly, leaning into his shoulder. "I'm so sorry about your grandma."

They sit there staring at the street and again, Toby marvels at how natural it feels. He doesn't feel pressured to fill each moment with witty banter or to pretend that he's fine when he isn't. He closes his eyes, grateful for a friend.

"Hey!" she exclaims suddenly, sitting upright. "Do you need help cleaning? I don't have to work until five."

Toby grins. "I'm almost done, but if you want to wipe some fridge shelves..."

"Done," she announces, standing up. "Where are the cloths?"

. . .

AFTER TAKING his hair elastic out and handing his keys over to the landlord, Toby walks next door to pick up Precious and a few things that might make Jo's room at Clara's feel more homey. This time, using a key, he walks through the front door and is immediately greeted by a ball of fluff around his ankles.

"Hi girl," he coos, reaching down to pet her. He walks into the kitchen—nearly tripping over her each time he takes a step—and pulls a can of cat food out of the cupboard.

"I get it!" he laughs, opening the can and placing the bowl on the floor. Purring, Precious begins gratefully lapping up the food.

"You're going to be a little out of sorts in a few minutes, but I promise Clara's house is nice. You'll like it eventually," he says, petting her back and then moving out of the kitchen to gather the other items.

Picking up the box he left in the entryway, he plucks the grey cat clock off of the wall and places it inside. Then he moves to the bedroom, scanning for other items that could be meaningful for Jo. A picture of her and Walter at their wedding catches his eye, and he picks it up. As he does so, something on the cluttered nightstand falls against the wall. Setting the box down on the bed, he falls to his hands and knees to look under the headboard. Using his phone as a flashlight, he scans the floor. Not surprisingly, more than one item appears to have found a home in the recesses of the carpet, and he reaches out to collect them.

He pulls back immediately, hitting something sharp. Checking for blood and not finding any, he reaches back under the bed, feeling around more gently this time. His fingers connect with pieces of something—likely broken. Carefully, he pulls the pieces into his hand and brings them into the light. In his hand he inspects the porcelain fragments, laying the tiny ball and chain out gently along his palm.

CHAPTER 40

That night, after all the hubbub has died down, Toby sits in a rocking chair next to Jo's hospice bed—a preemptive purchase by Clara that he is now extremely grateful for. It definitely beats the folding chair he would have been using. Jo's monitors hum next to her as she sleeps, exhausted by the move. Though he hasn't unloaded his belongings from the car, he at least attempted to settle Precious into her new living space. She immediately took shelter under Jo's bed and hasn't been seen since.

On a whim, Toby walks to the kitchen and retrieves her food and water dishes and slides them under the bed. She doesn't need to go hungry while she acclimates, he thinks. Sitting back in the chair, a slight panic rises in his chest. When Jo was in the hospital, everything seemed simple, but now...seeing her here in this bedroom...horrible images flash through his mind. Jo, gasping for air. Screaming in pain. And him not knowing how to help. He shudders and runs his hands through his hair.

She wanted this, he reminds himself. It's not like they had a cure for her and she can be comfortable here. Toby had made a grocery list with Clara days earlier so they could provide Jo with all of her favorites if and when she wakes up hungry. He even bought a few jello cups.

Not knowing what else to do, he pulls up the Kindle app on his phone and scrolls through the free, classic books he downloaded months ago. Finding the shortest one, he clicks on it and begins to read.

"Picture of Dorian Grey," he says out loud. "Let's see what this one's all about…"

Scrolling through the preface, he stops at the first chapter.

"Chapter 1," he says, clearing his throat. "The studio was filled with the rich odor of roses, and when the light summer wind stirred amidst the trees of the garden, there came through the open door the heavy scent of the lilac, or the more delicate perfume of the pink-flowering thorn..."

CLARA STANDS IN THE HALL, listening to Toby read. She allows her overstressed body to slide to the floor, resting her cheek against the wall.

"In the centre of the room, clamped to an upright easel, stood the full-length portrait of a young man of extraordinary personal beauty, and in front of it, some little distance away, was sitting the artist himself, Basil Hallward, whose sudden disappearance some years ago caused, at the time, such public excitement and gave rise to so many strange conjectures," Toby reads, his voice drifting into the hall.

"As the painter looked at the gracious and comely form he had so skillfully mirrored in his art, a smile of pleasure passed across his face, and seemed about to linger there. But he suddenly started up, and closing his eyes, placed his fingers upon the lids, as though he sought to imprison within his brain some curious dream from which he feared he might awake…"

Clara's eyelids droop as her breathing slows, imagining.

WAKING in the morning to her alarm, she starts upon noticing that she's in her bed, still dressed in her clothes from the night before. Feeling disheveled, she throws her blankets off and leans back to stretch her neck. She hastily reaches into her closet and picks out a shirt and slacks, then walks to the bathroom to shower.

Toby, though not needing to wake for anything in particular, is in the kitchen preparing breakfast. With no shift at Bob's today, he figured the least he could do was prepare breakfast. Though, who knows if Jo will even wake to enjoy it. Regardless, he cracks five eggs into a glass bowl and whisks them. Using a butter knife, he shaves off a pat of butter and drops it into the frying pan, already preheating on the stove. When it sizzles, he pours in the eggs, sprinkles salt and pepper over them, and immediately begins stirring.

"Hey," Clara says, walking into the kitchen, using a towel to scrunch her hair.

"That was fast," Toby laughs. "Didn't I just hear your door open, like, five minutes ago?"

"I think it was closer to ten, but yes, I do take fast showers. If I don't get in and out, I'll stay there for an hour."

Toby grins.

"Did you put me in my bed last night?"

"I did, hope that's okay. You didn't look very comfortable slumped against the wall like that."

"Thanks," she says. "I didn't expect to sack out. What were you reading anyway?"

"Oh, yeah. I figured I could read to Jo at night. Not sure if she can actually hear anything, but—"

"No, I think it's a great idea," Clara assures him.

"Last night I was reading 'The Picture of Dorian Grey', by Oscar Wilde I think?"

"Mmmm, that's right. I haven't read that in ages. Forgot how it started."

"I like it so far," Toby says, pulling the pan from the stove and setting it on a hot pad on the counter.

"Eggs?" he asks, reaching for the bowls.

"Sure, thanks."

"I'll save some out for Jo if she wakes up. If not, I'm sure Precious will eat them," he chuckles.

"Don't give that cat diarrhea or I'm going to lose it," Clara warns and Toby laughs out loud.

"I'm pretty sure she's eaten way worse than this," he retorts. Taking his share of eggs, he sits next to his sister at the table. "Oh, I forgot to tell you," he says excitedly, suddenly remembering. "When I was picking up Jo's things, I dropped something behind the bed. I reached back there to get it and ended up finding something I think you'll be interested in." He stands up and rushes to his room, returning with his hands cupped. Gently, he sets the pieces of the bell on the table.

"No way," Clara breathes. "This was behind her bed?"

Toby nods. "She must have knocked it off the nightstand at some point. I'm surprised it broke, honestly. It must have hit the baseboard or something on the way down."

"So. Brett's probably not a thief."

"But he is liable for burying a dead body in a public place," Toby says.

Clara holds a hand over her mouth to prevent egg from spewing all over the table.

CHAPTER 41

A beeping sound wakes Toby, and he jumps out of the rocking chair, nearly falling over in the process. Light streams in through the window, so he couldn't have been out for that long. Frantically searching for the source of the problem, he breathes a sigh of relief when he sees that Jo's IV bag is empty. He takes his time placing a new bag, making sure the tube is connected securely. Then he moves back to the chair.

Jo shifts in the bed. Toby opens his phone, attempting to look busy so he isn't staring at her as she wakes.

"Toby?" Jo whispers, her voice hoarse. She remembers his name.

"Hey, Jo, it's me," he says. Precious, hearing Jo's voice, slides out from under the bed and looks up curiously. Not able to stay away, she alights to the bed and Jo jumps back in shock.

"Oh!" she exclaims, reaching her hand out to pet the cat. Precious purrs and rubs up against her arm. Jo smiles at Toby gratefully.

"Of course, we couldn't leave her at your place. I told you she missed you," Toby says, grinning.

"How long—?" she asks, coughing slightly.

Looking at the feline clock on the wall, he answers, "You've been sleeping for about...eighteen hours, I think? Can I get you something to eat? Drink?"

She nods.

"I made eggs."

Jo smiles, and Toby moves to the kitchen. When he returns—with a bowl of eggs and a glass of Jo's favorite orange juice—he finds Jo looking out the window, with Precious asleep on her lap.

"Hmmm. Not sure where to put this. We don't really have a fancy table like at the hospital," he says, scanning the room for options. "Oh!" he says, setting the food on the dresser. "I think Clara has some TV stands, let me go check."

Finding them in the hall closet, he quickly sets one up next to Jo's bed.

"It's a little low," he chuckles, but Jo waves him off. Turning, he retrieves the eggs and juice and sets them next to her.

"Just don't spill on Clara's carpet, she might kill me."

Jo begins to move her arms, trying to reach the bowl, but can only manage to shift a few inches. Nobody had been sure whether she would have mobility or not, but it doesn't look promising.

"Here," Toby offers. "Your body has been through a lot, let me help you."

Jo looks at him, her eyes wide. "Poison!" she gets out, craning her neck.

"Ah," Toby says nodding. "You're right. That's why your arms aren't moving. Well, this food is poison free. At least it won't make things worse," he says, sitting next to her and picking up the bowl. He spoons a small bite of eggs into her mouth and waits for her to chew. Swallowing takes some time, but she manages.

She sighs and opens her mouth for another bite.

"Glad you like it," Toby says, suppressing a laugh, and filling the fork a second time. They follow this routine until all the eggs are gone. Though she struggles to drink, the straw in the orange juice seems to allow her to get small sips down.

"Too late," she says when she finishes swallowing her last bite.

Toby's eyebrows furrow. "What do you mean?"

"Too much poison," she says, her voice hoarse.

"You think it's too late?" Toby confirms, and Jo nods emphatically. "Why do you think that?" he asks.

She motions at her body, shaking her head.

Toby breathes deeply, clenching his teeth to keep his eyes from welling up. "I guess we'll see. I'll keep making your favorite foods and you just keep resting, okay?"

Jo nods, her eyes fearful. "Toby," she whispers, motioning for him to come closer. He leans in, pulling the chair with him.

"Cereal box," she says.

"Do you want cereal?" Toby asks, confused. She just ate a lot, how could she be hungry already?

"My cereal box," she repeats.

"Do you want a special kind of cereal?"

Jo nods, gripping his sleeve with surprising intensity. "My house."

"Okay," he nods. "I can go over there at some point and get it. Can it wait for a few days?" he asks.

She nods again. "Inside."

Toby shifts on the bed. "Got it. I think," he says, regarding her quizzically. Jo slumps back on her pillow, exhausted from the exchange. She closes her eyes and Toby watches her chest rise and fall as she finally relaxes.

THAT EVENING, Jo is awake when he walks in to check on her. The Simply Living workers were there all afternoon giving her a sponge bath and shifting her position. Toby hasn't seen the bruising yet, and he hopes he won't have to.

"Hey, do you mind if I read for a while?" he asks her, taking his usual seat. Precious is eating out of her food bowl under the bed, making a clinking sound as she digs for the kibble. Jo searches the room, looking for the source of the sound. "It's Precious," Toby explains. "She's probably missing her wet food. I'll get her some before I go to bed," he promises.

Jo nods and then watches him as he reads, her eyelids already beginning to droop.

"'Mr. Dorian Gray is in the studio, sir,' said the butler, coming into the garden.

'You must introduce me now,' cried Lord Henry, laughing. The painter turned to his servant, who stood blinking in the sunlight.

'Ask Mr. Gray to wait, Parker: I shall be in in a few moments.' The man bowed and went up the walk.

Then he looked at Lord Henry. 'Dorian Gray is my dearest friend,' he said. 'He has a simple and a beautiful nature. Your aunt was quite right in what she said of him. Don't spoil him. Don't try to influence him. Your influence would be bad. The world is wide, and has many marvelous people in it. Don't take away from me the one person who gives to my art whatever charm it possesses: my life as an artist depends on him. Mind, Harry, I trust you.' He spoke very slowly, and the words seemed wrung out of him almost against his will."

"What is it?" Jo asks sluggishly.

"Oscar Wilde," Toby answers. "Would you like something else?"

She shakes her head. "Thank you," she manages, her head sinking into the pillow. Lying there—her white hair making a halo around her head—she looks peaceful and almost heavenly. Toby reads to the end of the chapter and then silently slips out of the room.

CHAPTER 42

Toby walks through the back hall, about to cash out for the night. Though it hadn't been slow, it certainly wasn't a good night for tips. Still, working a shift was a great distraction from everything going on at home.

"Headed home?" Abby says, walking past him to put in an order at the dock.

"Yep, are you closing tonight?"

"You know it," she says. "It's pretty slow, though. I'll probably just end up eating chocolate cake with the cooks."

Toby feels a slight pang of jealousy, wishing he didn't have to miss out on that.

"What are you doing this weekend?" Abby asks, putting her card back in her apron.

"Besides watching my grandma? I'm wide open," he chuckles.

"I am planning to go up to the rose gardens with a friend from high school and hike around the park a bit. Want to come?"

"The rose gardens? I haven't been up there yet," he says. "I'd love to, it just depends—"

"No, I get it," she says. "Here, hand me your phone."

He pulls it out of his pocket and hands it to her. She types something and then hands it back.

"You just sent me a text," she says, flashing a cheesy smile.

Toby grins. "I'll let you know if I can make it."

She walks back to the dining room, her dark hair bouncing around her shoulders. Looking down at his phone, Toby realizes that he has three missed calls. All from Clara. His heart begins to pound as he calls her back.

"Hey, Clara, sorry I missed your call. My shift just ended," Toby explains, holding the phone to his ear and taking off his apron.

"Clara?" he asks, not hearing anything on the other end of the line.

Clara sucks in an audible breath. "Toby, you need to get home."

Panic grips him and he freezes. "Is Jo—?"

"Just come home right now," she says, sniffling between words. He hangs up, grabs his keys and rushes out of the restaurant.

SCREECHING to a halt in front of the house, he hastily puts the car in park and jumps out to the street, not locking it as usual. Running up the walkway, he throws open the front door and bounds up the steps. Clara waits for him in the hallway. Her face is contorted and she points toward Jo's bedroom.

Toby enters cautiously, barely finding room to stand as two workers hover over Jo. One is holding an oxygen mask over her mouth and nose.

"What's—" Toby asks, but stops when a gloved hand is held up in his face. He stands against the wall, waiting as his heart hammers in his chest. Eventually the men look at each other and speak behind their masks. While he can't understand what they're saying, he watches them remove the equipment from Jo's body—one tube at a time. He watches her chest rise and fall, so subtly that it's scary.

"I'm sorry to cut you off," one of the nurse's addresses him, pulling down his mask.

"No, it's alright, I understand."

"We did everything we could, but...she's only got a few more minutes. We'll get out of here," he says, his eyes empathetic. "You may hear an alarm when she passes. Just hit this button right here to turn off the machine. We'll wait outside. If you could call us…"

Toby nods, wiping a tear from his cheek. Clara joins him in the room as soon as they exit. Precious pokes her head out from under the bed and, ignoring Toby and Clara, jumps to Jo's lap. Jo lies still except for the slight movement of her breath.

Her eyelids flutter, but her eyes remain closed. Clara reaches for Toby's hand as he leans over the bed. Pulling her forward, he picks up Jo's hand and holds it between theirs.

They stand in that sacred space as Jo's chest rises and falls. Rises and falls. What he would give for one more word from her. Some sort of closure, anything, he thinks. How cruel that even when she was awake, she couldn't actually share what was on her mind. And why didn't he go sooner to get the cereal she wanted? He berates himself for not rushing over immediately after she asked and tears begin to form at the corner of his eyes.

Her chest rises and falls. Rises and falls. And then sits still. Precious curls up in the space between Jo's shoulder and neck. Toby hits the button.

CHAPTER 43

The next morning, Toby pulls up in front of Jo's old townhome. The drizzly rain fits his mood as he walks to the front door and steps inside. Walking directly into the kitchen and opening the cupboard, Toby reaches for the cereal boxes and hesitates. Why would she have wanted old shredded wheat? Puzzled, he pulls down the boxes of identical cereal and flips open the tops. Two of the bags are unopened, but the third...he looks closer. No bag is evident, only a rolled up piece of paper. Taking a deep breath, he pulls it out and flattens it on the countertop. Realization dawns as he begins to read.

"Herein lies the last Will and Testament…" he scans, bypassing the typical legal jargon and stopping a paragraph or so down. "I don't have much personally to bequeath, besides my cat and my car, both of which go to Toby, my neighbor. Everything else is really Walter's and shall be divided pursuant to instructions left with Mr. William Schwartz."

Toby stares at the paper. In light script at the bottom of the letterhead, he finds a phone number and an address.

. . .

THE WIPERS of the Buick swish back and forth, trying to keep up with the torrential downpour this morning. Arriving at the office building just a few blocks away, Toby parks and runs toward the main entrance, holding the paper close to his chest. Inside, he shakes off his jacket and finds a sign directing him to the fourth floor. It occurs to him that he probably should have called Clara after finding the document, but she's at work...and he's too curious to wait.

Stepping off the elevator, he finds himself in a modest office waiting room. One sofa rests along the wall, and a slim woman with grey hair sits at a reception desk. She smiles at him as he approaches.

"Hi," he says, setting the will on her desk. "My grandmother passed and it seems Mr. Schwartz helped her with this."

Putting on her glasses, she pulls the paper toward her and inspects it.

"Would you like to discuss this with Bill?" she asks, handing it back to him.

"Yes, if that's okay. I don't have an appointment— "

"That's fine, he's in the office today. I'll call him."

Toby nods and takes a seat, his knee bouncing involuntarily. I'm only twenty-one, he thinks, and I'm meeting with an executor of a will? Is this what happened when Mom died? He imagines all of the logistics that must have taken place without his knowing.

Every memory of that time feels cloudy to him. He must have visited his mom in the hospital almost daily, yet he can only truly envision one instance...

. . .

"Toby," Grandma Jo says, reaching out and pulling him close. Clara pokes his ribs from behind and he wriggles against her arms, wanting to continue their game of tag.

"Clara," Jo says sternly, "sit here, please. We really can't be running around in the waiting room."

"But why? There's nobody here," she whines.

"Clara, you're eleven years old. I need you to be an example to your brother," she pleads. Clara sits, though she isn't happy about it.

"Toby," Grandma continues, "I need to talk to you before we go in to see Mom." Toby nods, leaning against her knees. "She's going to look different this time."

"How?" he asks, confused.

"She's going to be hooked up to a bunch of different tubes and machines, it might look a little scary."

"Why does she need to stay in the hospital?" he asks. "I want her to come home."

"I know, we all do," Jo sighs. "She's sick, and those tubes are giving her medicine to help her feel better."

"Will she get better?" Toby asks, his eyes pleading.

"No," Clara says under her breath.

"Clara," Grandma Jo says, turning abruptly, "we don't know that. All we can do is hope."

"Toby?"

He lifts his head, jolting back to the present. A stout, balding man walks into the waiting room and thrusts out his hand. Toby stands, shaking it.

"What's your name, son?" he asks, his voice strong and commanding.

"Toby," he answers.

"Well, Toby, come with me," he says, ushering him behind the desk and down a short hallway to his office. "So you are the one that Jo talked of so highly," he says, rounding his desk and sitting in a leather rolling chair.

"She did?" he asks, sliding the paper across the wooden surface.

"I don't even need to look at this," he says, waving it off. "We wrote this up so recently, I've still got it memorized," he chuckles.

"How did you know Jo?" Toby asks.

"Well I didn't until she showed up here one day."

"On her own?"

"That's right," he says, leaning back with his hands behind his head. "I often do pro bono work through the library and someone there gave her my info. She marched right over here and told me she needed a will."

"Did she pay you?"

"She insisted."

Toby grins. "That sounds like her. She...wasn't always quite herself," he explains. "I guess I'm wondering how she was able to give you all the information you needed to deal with her estate."

"She seemed perfectly lucid to me," Bill insists. "We got on the phone together with her care provider and they were able to give me account information. Though she didn't want to see the balances," he chuckles.

Toby sighs. "That sounds like her, too. I'm not quite sure why I rushed over here. I guess I needed to see how this all came about," he says, looking around the small office. "I do have one question, though. Do you know if there's any sort of provision in her instructions for funeral expenses?"

"When you showed up, I assumed she had passed," Bill says gently.

"Yesterday," Toby says. "My sister and I are trying to sort all of this out. Jo didn't have life insurance—"

"Those policies don't usually cover past a certain age," Bill explains.

"Right," Toby agrees, standing. Even mentioning money—or worse, asking for it—makes him itch all over. "Well, I'm not sure what instructions Jo gave you, but if you see anything about funeral provisions, please let me know? I appreciate you taking the time to help sort this out. I really don't have a clue about these things."

"You were her neighbor, right?" Bill asks.

Toby nods, adjusting his glasses. "I'm actually her grandson," he admits. "Jo...she had dementia and she wasn't really open to people claiming to be related to her. My sister figured that out the hard way. My mom—her daughter—died when we were both young and our Dad didn't really make an effort to keep in touch with her family. We didn't know much about her...anyway, we wanted to get to know her. If that makes sense?" he stammers, fidgeting with his phone in his pocket. Saying it out loud sounds much stranger than he expected. "Anyway, I decided to find a way to be her friend."

Bill nods. "Well, I think you succeeded," he states, turning to the filing cabinet behind him.

Assuming he's moved on to more important things, Toby turns to leave.

"Just wait a second there, son. I'd like you to see this."

Turning and taking a seat, Toby waits patiently while Bill rifles through files.

"There it is," he says finally, pulling out a manila folder and slapping it on the desk. Putting on his glasses, he turns over a few loose leaf pages and then turns the entire folder toward Toby.

"Read that paragraph there," he instructs. Toby follows his finger and scans the text.

After a few moments, he looks up. "It seems like this is saying that Jo's trust goes first to the eldest surviving family member," Toby says, blinking. "This doesn't make any sense. My sister said something about all of her money going to a cat shelter."

Bill laughs, resting his hand on his belly. "She did have that in her previous will, but it's void at this point. I have a copy of it in her file if you'd like to see it."

"No, that's okay. But why did she change it?" Toby asks, scratching his head.

Bill smiles. "Not sure. But she did," he says. "Is it you?"

Toby shakes his head, "No, but it's my sister." He sits back down in the chair. "From what Jo figured, she didn't have much. Is there enough in there to at least cover the funeral?"

Again, Bill's belly shakes as he chuckles, pulling out another file. "Oh, I think you'll find there's a little more than that."

Toby leaves the office building and steps into the rain, still in total disbelief. Why would she have changed her will? And how did she have that much left in her trust? If she was smart enough to work with a lawyer, she must have done her due diligence to figure out how her money would be distributed if left up to the state. Could she have suspected—? Toby shakes his head. No, there's no way. She would have said something. Wouldn't she?

Arriving at the Buick completely drenched, he slips into the seat. What had the last twenty years been like for Jo? Through his eight-year-old eyes, she had been the one keeping him from his mom. All he wanted was *her* and instead, he got...her. That must have been devastating. Tears well in his eyes as he thinks about the times he threw fits, the times he refused to speak to her, the times he screamed in his room, begging for her to let his mom come home. Then he would wake up in the morning to eggs and orange juice, his backpack ready on the chair...

He grips the steering wheel and allows his head to fall against it, his shoulders shaking. As the rain pounds against the windows, he gives in to his emotions and weeps.

When his breathing normalizes, he lifts his head and slumps back in the seat, wiping his face with his hands. Feeling lighter than he has in weeks, he sits up and puts the key in the ignition. This is my car now, he realizes. Time to grow up. He opens his phone and searches the address for the closest DMV.

CHAPTER 44

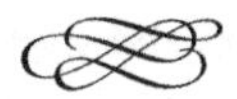

"So what's your plan now?" Clara asks, sitting across from Toby in the kitchen.

He leans forward, folding his arms around his plate. "I don't know, honestly. Get through the funeral first—is Dad coming out for that?"

"Not sure," Clara says, taking a bite of beef stroganoff.

"It's going to be small," Toby comments.

"That's okay, she would've wanted it that way," Clara states.

Toby nods. "So, get through that and then...move out of here so you can have your house back—"

"You can stay as long as you need," she insists.

"I know, but I've at least got to get that litter box out of here," he teases. "Seriously, though, I think I'm ready to move on. The semester starts in a couple months. I could move back to Madison, get a job—"

"Is that what you want?"

Toby nods, "I think it is. I still have some research to do, but I have an idea of what I want to study."

"Healthcare, perhaps?"

His cheeks flush. "Perhaps," he admits. "I still have to find out if I'm allowed to switch majors at this point."

"And if not?"

"Then...I might be really overqualified for my next position," he laughs. "Hey, did you ever get to talk to Simply Living about Brett?"

"I didn't really need to," she sighs, setting her fork down. "I looked into all of the complaints. He does get more of them than anyone else, but I think it's his bedside manner. He just doesn't inspire confidence in the elderly," she says.

"So they don't like him? That's it?"

"Seems that way," Clara agrees. "I actually took a look at Jo's ledger."

"You did?" Toby asks, surprised.

"When I was over there cataloging her things I noticed it. I compared it with Simply Living's records and they were pretty darn close. It was off by a few dollars here and there, but nothing major."

"So why did Jo think the amounts were always changing," he questions.

Clara nods. "Tob, you have to understand, these patients don't understand that we don't actually have access to their full banking information. The statement we show clients only reflects the balance for their expenses that month. Simply Living has access to their full estate, but not us. Our job is to help them utilize that stipend to pay their bills, purchase any necessities, and make sure nothing slides through the cracks. There's no way I could have known how much Jo had in there. And no wonder she was so upset every time she saw her balance," Clara explains.

"So the problem is communication," Toby muses. "If we could have helped her understand that, then we could have looked into helping her manage her actual trust. But, what I don't understand is...if she went to that lawyer, she must have been able to access her account. Right?"

"You'd think so..." Clara says. "But maybe she only had the paperwork. I wouldn't be surprised if she didn't know how to find her actual balance."

"True," Toby agrees.

Clara pulls a legal pad from the kitchen junk drawer.

"What are you doing?" Toby asks.

"Just writing a few notes for my next meeting. I'm going to suggest that we do a workshop on patient financials. Hopefully streamline this process so there isn't so much confusion."

"And maybe assign *anyone but Brett* to discuss this with dementia patients," Toby says, incredulous. "Why in the world has he been the go-to guy?"

Clara throws up her hands, "I have no idea!" she laughs. "I definitely brought that up with my supervisor already."

Toby takes another bite of noodles, and Clara grins. "What about Abby?"

Toby motions to his full mouth and refuses to answer.

"I see how it is," Clara laughs. "Just for the record, I like her."

"I do too," he says, his mouth still full of food.

"You could work here for another few weeks or so, sign up for classes? You do have a good job here, after all," she says. "And...even if you didn't. I just came into a little bit of money. I might be willing to spot you," she teases.

Toby shakes his head. "I'm never going to hear the end of this, am I?" He looks to the door and sees Precious sauntering in toward her food dish. "Well she's mine," Toby laughs, pointing at the cat. "So there."

Clara grins. "Seriously. You think you may want to stick around for a bit?"

"That wouldn't be the worst, I guess," he admits. "I'll think about it."

"You do that," Clara says. She reaches down and pets the cat, then turns to the sink. Filling it with soapy water, she picks up a pan and begins to scrub.

THE END

ALSO BY CINDY GUNDERSON

Tier Trilogy (Tier 1, Tier 2, Tier 3)

I Can't Remember

Let's Try This Again, But This Time in Paris

Holly Bough Cottage

The New Year's Party

www.CindyGunderson.com

Instagram: @CindyGWrites

Facebook: @CindyGWrites

ABOUT THE AUTHOR

Cindy is first and foremost mother to her four beautiful children and wife to her charming and handsome husband, Scott. She is a musician, a homeschooler, a gardener, an athlete, an actor, a lover of Canadian chocolate, and most recently, a writer.

Cindy grew up in Airdrie, AB, Canada, but has lived most of her adult life between California and Colorado. She currently resides in the Denver metro area. Cindy graduated from Brigham Young University in 2005 with a B.S. in Psychology, minoring in Business. She serves actively within her church and community and is always up for a new adventure.